an insiders novel
take it off

take it off

an insiders novel
by j. minter

BLOOMSBURY

BLOOMSBURY

Published by Bloomsbury Publishing, New York, London, and Berlin
Distributed to the trade by Holtzbrinck Publishers

Library of Congress Cataloging-in-Publication Data
Minter, J.
Take it off : an insiders novel / by J. Minter.—1st U.S. ed.
  p. cm.
Summary: Four wealthy Manhattan teenagers find love and adventure in the Mediterranean when they join an Ocean Term cruise.
  ISBN-10: 1-58234-994-0 (pbk.)
  ISBN-13: 978-1-58234-994-7 (pbk.)
 [1. Cruise ships—Fiction. 2. Mediterranean Sea—Fiction.] I. Title
PZ7.M67334Tak 2005   [Fic]—dc22   2005040532

Produced by Alloy Entertainment
151 West 26th Street
New York, NY 10011

First U.S. Edition 2005
Printed in the U.S.A.
10 9 8 7 6 5 4 3 2 1

Bloomsbury Publishing, Children's Books, U.S.A.
175 Fifth Avenue, New York, NY 10010

All papers used by Bloomsbury Publishing are natural, recyclable products made from wood grown in well-managed forests. The manufacturing processes conform to the environmental regulations of the country of origin.

for ASG

Picture yourself on a boat on an ocean . . .

The single best thing about life on my dad's new wife's yacht (you remember, don't you?) was that, for a short time, almost everyone I really care about was close by and easy to locate. That's what the last thirteen days were like, and it's what the next two weeks should hold in store, too. Except now we're on an even bigger boat, with tons of girls.

Okay, let's make a long, twisted story short: My dad married a woman rich even by our standards named Penelope Isquierdo Santana Suttwilley (or PISS, as I like to think of her). She's got a yacht, one of those two-hundred-fifty-foot deals that you can live on, with a crew and everything, and she and my dad decided to have their honeymoon on it. They invited me and PISS's son, Serge, and they told me I could bring whichever friend I wanted, which ended up being all of them: Arno, Patch, David, and Mickey. Don't even ask me how that happened.

Our days of cruising had their ups and downs, of course. David never got used to the movement of the ocean. In fact, he looked a little like the Jolly Green Giant with the flu from day one. And then Arno started yelling "Where's the bucket!" whenever he saw him, and that, as you can imagine, got old fast. Mickey took to diving off the yacht unexpectedly. We'd hear a loud scream: "I got my mind on my money and my money on my . . . *yeeaggh!*" and turn to see a bright pair of Vilebrequin floral swim trunks lying on the deck, followed shortly by a loud splash.

Needless to say, all the screaming and name-calling gave my new stepmom a case of the nerves, as she told us many times, and she was forced to up her sedative intake. Her nerves gave me nerves, but still, most of the time I could see all my friends from wherever I was standing, and I liked that.

I'd never seen Patch in a more natural setting. He and the captain's son would fish off the back of the boat and drink Coronas in the afternoon, and then meet up with rest of us for hors d'oeuvres at cocktail hour, and the chef would cook up the fish they'd caught for dinner. And even I—who had no choice but to deal with this jet set Latin spitfire of a new stepmother, and with having to have "talks" with my dad (who is basically a wealthy deadbeat)—even *I* was almost perfectly content. Even with Mickey's erratic diving, I knew there was no place for him to go but back to the big cabin we all shared (unless he got eaten by a shark or something totally awful, which was a possibility I wouldn't even think about). And that contented feeling pretty much went for all of my friends, too.

Plus, the whole yacht/white deck shoes/Persol sunglasses/champagne look is something I really got into. Before we set sail from Miami, Dad took me and Serge on a shopping spree to Gucci and Neiman Marcus in Merrick Park, and I got V-neck navy sweaters and some white pants, and the whole look was very sailor-at-rest.

Of course, the shopping was what cued me in that there was going to be some kind of trouble. That's when I met Serge. We all drove over together in the vintage Karmann Ghia that Dad keeps in the lower level of the yacht, and the whole way Serge kept sort of squealing, "Barneys Co-op Mee-AH-mee!" But I'm at Barneys all the time in New York, so why would I want to go there? Anyway, to make matters worse, he had this greasy spiked hair that had a sort of unintentional Hives look, and he was wearing oversized wraparound shades and a collared shirt that was open to nipple level, revealing a few curly black chest hairs. This is what we call *Eurotrash* in Manhattan. You find a lot of these people hanging around the NYU area chain-smoking and looking like they've been up all night doing E and talking about life and ratting up their hair. I got over that scene back when I was a sophomore.

After my new stepbrother got his way and we left Barneys, he pushed down his wraparounds, looked at me, and said, "By the way, Joan-a-tin, nobody calls me *Serge* but Mama. You can call me *Rohb*."

Serge—I mean, Rob—hated being on the boat, and all the way through the Caribbean he sulked and holed up belowdecks and chain-smoked. That's how he and David initially hit it off. They both complained about the smell of the ocean, so while the rest of us enjoyed lazy evenings watching the sunset turn the horizon into golden explosions, they'd be downstairs complaining about how much everything sucked for them.

David tolerated Rob's smoking because Rob tolerated the endless videos of Peja Stojakovic's layups that David had to watch before the beginning of the next basketball season. They watched Peja, inhaled secondhand smoke, and turned pale while the rest of us browned.

After ten days, once we'd lost count of the picturesque seaside villages and breathtaking natural phenomena, and after we'd visited with the Venezuelan half of PISS's crazy family, we arrived back in Miami. The night before Dad and PISS flew back to London, he put in a call to Mom. When he handed me the phone, she explained that they had "reached a new level of peace" and that to prove it she was going to have Rob stay at our house, in my brother Ted's room. It might have annoyed me, except that I was about to sail across the Atlantic with a full crew to pamper me and my friends, and I didn't have to even think about any crazy parent drama until the program was over. I was feeling pretty freakin' great about everything.

Oh, wait.

Maybe you're wondering, What program? Where am I? And how'd I get here? Put it this way: Blame my mom. She decided to bring up all that junior year, precollege anxiety while I was packing to go on what I thought would be the worst trip of my life. (I had no reason to assume the trip would be so relaxing and awesome at this point, and she really didn't, either.)

Flashback to right before I went down to Miami. I was sitting with my mom, and as usual, I was about to get some weird, weird news.

"Jonathan," my mom said, sitting on my bed and giving me her serious face. She took a sip of the eggnog that was left over from our Christmas party. "The Grobarts were just telling me about this winter break precollege program. It's on a cruise ship called the *Ariadne*, and you board in the Mediterranean, so it would be perfect timing with this trip you're going on for your father's honeymoon. When the yacht makes its return trip to Greece for winter storage, you can stay aboard. It would be really good for you, a little something different to put on those college apps. Maybe your friends could go with you. Think about it, okay?"

She put a brochure on my bedspread, and then said, "I'll leave you alone," like she was doing me a favor.

The brochure said: *Ocean Term: Be a Student of*

the World, and it had a glossy picture of a good-looking girl sitting next to an old, sun-wrinkled man. They were both laughing. The caption said: *Stephanie Rayder, Sicily, Winter '02.* Inside, it described how, for two weeks, a "diverse, international" student body of three hundred teenagers would sail from Athens, through the Mediterranean, around the Iberian Peninsula, and on to London. Along the way, we would study classics, history, and sailing. This would provide us with "innumerable character-building challenges," including an overnight survival test. It all sounded kind of earnest and boring, and I had been planning on coming home quick after my dad's honeymoon, because things had just started to get good again with Flan Flood and me. Besides, I almost never leave Manhattan, so the idea of four weeks away kind of freaked me out.

But then, unbelievably, everyone in the group of guys I've been best friends with since fifth grade said they might be down to go, and it started sounding fun.

Patch was easy to convince, because he grew up on a sailboat and has never been comfortable in a conventional classroom. This was kind of like asking him to go to heaven. And Arno's parents,

13

who are famously crazy New York art collectors, had just confessed that their marriage was a sham and so his whole family life was crumbling very publicly. There had been some gossip column chattering about it, and everywhere Arno went, people stared at him, and not in the usual good way. I couldn't blame the guy for wanting to blow town. Mickey and his girlfriend, Philippa Frady, had finally admitted to each other that their relationship was just too intense, and had tentatively called it quits, so Mickey was this constant streak of destructive, single-dude energy. He took one look at the girl on the brochure and he was sold. And David? Well, David never really knew how to negotiate New York without us, so he was in, too. Arno, Patch, David, Mickey, and me, Jonathan. It was almost like having just about everything I like about Manhattan come with me.

I suspect that, besides all that, we were needing more time off from New York than we were letting on. The past couple of months have been filled with more secrets and lies than I can possibly keep straight, but the big ones go about like this:

1) Back in the '80s, when everyone was

making and losing money like crazy, my dad stole money (okay, a lot of money) from just about all of my friends' parents. I spent about two weeks slinking around like a criminal, and it cost me a girl I was pretty into.

2) It turned out that Arno's dad, Alec Wildenburger, is gay, and that:

3) Arno's mom, Allie, was having an affair with Ricardo Pardo, who is a rich and famous artist who is:

   a) represented by Alec Wildenburger, and

   b) also the father of Mickey, Arno's best friend.

4) Meanwhile, Mickey's mom/Ricardo's wife was having an affair with the guy painting my apartment. Which brings us back to:

5) Me. And I, unfortunately, still have a secret. Or, at least, I hope it's still somewhat of a secret. Before we left, I acted like this totally emotionally stunted dude with Flan, and things may be worse between us than I'm letting on.

6) I especially hope that Patch doesn't know about that, since Flan is his little sister. And she's in eighth grade. Patch doesn't really

have any secrets, besides being generally elusive. But something new in his personality seems to be emerging: He acts more mature and capable, and this change in him has us all more twisted out than everything in 1 through 5 combined.

So, with all of that as recent history, you can see why a couple extra weeks away seemed like a good idea. The plan was for us all to go straight to Ocean Term from my dad's honeymoon. I figured I'd need another vacation after a vacation like that, anyway. And that's how we ended up here, on the *Ariadne*, with a whole lot of other kids. They aren't really a "diverse, international" group—mostly they're Brits and Americans. But that's okay. We can still write it that way on our college applications. And, before I tell you anything else, I should warn you that this trip is going to throw us challenges that that brochure didn't even *hint* at.

Smooth sailing for Arno

The students of Ocean Term were supposed to divide up into their orientation groups and sit quietly in clusters on the deck of the *Ariadne*. It was their third night on the ship, and they had already learned how to turn the evening lectures into covert parties in plain view. There was no moon, and the program director, Roger Barker, was explaining the myths behind various constellations. He used a microphone, and looked at the sky as he spoke and gestured grandly. Meanwhile, the kids carried on quiet conversations and snuck from one group to another. Arno Wildenburger took a flask of Jack Daniels out of his jacket pocket and took a sip.

Arno's group's RA was a British anarchist and anti-globalization protester who called himself Loki. He was more than willing to look the other way.

Already the students were forming cliques and hooking up with each other. It all seemed sort of immature to Arno, like the New Hampshire summer camp that his parents had sent him to in junior high. Still, a two-week party on a cruise ship with three hundred other kids couldn't be an entirely bad thing.

On the first night, Arno had been irritated that he was stranded in this group with none of his New York crew. But he didn't mind so much anymore. Patch had already become the most talked-about kid on the trip, and of course Arno hated that. Apparently, during Patch's orientation group's day trip through ancient ruins on Delos, Patch had caught some looters trying to make off with the head of an ancient statue of Aphrodite. The island's team of archaeologists had practically asked if they could keep Patch, they loved him so much. And stuff between Mickey and Arno was strained anyway, because of all the parental entanglements that came out around Thanksgiving. They had been steering clear, as it were, since then. There was Jonathan's mooning over Flan, too, which had gotten a little bit annoying. And, oh yes, there was another reason that Arno was glad to be going it alone.

He'd met Suki Davison bright and early Monday morning, during their first orientation meeting. She was wearing a sticker that said: HELLO MY NAME IS: SUKI, BERKELEY, CA. Nobody else had a sticker like that, and Arno couldn't decide whether this made her cute or geeky. (By that afternoon, when at least ten other girls had managed to get the same kind of sticker and Suki's had disappeared, he decided she was pretty freaking cool.) She was half Japanese and half California WASP, and she had long dark hair and bangs cut in a straight line over her eyes. There was a small tattoo of a Japanese character on her shoulder, and when they went around in a circle and told the group something about themselves, she said, "Yeah, that *is* a tattoo, and yeah, it is my name in Japanese. Now none of you have to ask me about it ever again."

She wasn't the kind of cool girl that Arno was used to hanging out with in New York. But she had that sort of laid-back California thing going on that made her a most-desirable in this kind of alternative education setting. When Loki asked if anyone had any questions or problems during orientation, her hand shot up and she said, "I am very concerned that Ocean Term has decided to serve meat in its cafeteria. I don't want to impose my views on anyone else, but I'd just like to say that financially supporting the meat industry seems contradictory to everything this program stands for." It wasn't cool, but Arno had to admit it was sort of sassy. Besides, she had really long legs, and Arno, who was six one, thought he made a better-looking couple with a girl who was almost as tall as he was.

Arno snuck another sip of the Jack and leaned toward Suki, who was sitting cross-legged next to him and listening to the lecture. He was close enough that when he breathed deeply, and then exhaled, the hair around her ear moved slightly. She smelled exotic and familiar at once, like the perfect mix of incense and girl's skin.

"It's pretty cold out," he said, even though it wasn't remotely chilly. "You want a nip?"

"Thanks," she said, turning her face so that her nose almost touched Arno's. After she took a sip, she looked back up at the stars. Barker was saying, "And if you look to your left you can see Dorado, and you're lucky, because you can only see it in January, and . . ."

"This is probably where I should ask you about your sign," he said, "but that's not really how I do things."

She smiled. "That's good," she said, and took another swig before giving the flask back to him. "You're from New York, right? I bet you've never even seen stars like this."

He looked up. The sky above them glittered with stars. "No," he said, "guess not. So . . . what do kids do for fun in Berkeley?"

"Probably about the same as you and your friends do," she said. He laughed, because he doubted it. "You know, party, cause drama."

"I'd like to get in some drama with you."

"Yeah, that might be a good time."

Barker had finished his talk and was winding up his evening messages.

"I'm very pleased with our exploration of Delos," he was saying. "I'd like to congratulate one of Ocean Term's students in particular. Yesterday, he was able to stop bandits from stealing an ancient and sacred piece of art. Patch Flood, ladies and gentleman." Patch stood up sheepishly next to him and half waved at the crowd. Everyone murmured. Barker continued, "You could all learn a little something from him about the importance of embracing and protecting ancient cultures. Now, we'll reach Sicily by morning, and there will be day trips tomorrow for those interested . . ."

"That's one of my guys from New York," Arno said to Suki.

"Really? Barker thinks he's pretty special."

"Yeah, well . . ." Arno stopped when he saw Mickey, on elbows and knees, coming toward them.

"My group sucks," Mickey hissed.

Loki looked over and glared at them to be more quiet. Apparently anarchy had its limits.

"Suki Davison, meet Mickey Pardo," Arno said. He wasn't sure if he was more annoyed that Mickey was interrupting what was happening with Suki, or that he was trying to act like they were totally cool, when obviously they'd been sort of distanced for weeks, even on

Jonathan's stepmom's awesome yacht.

He also didn't really want Suki meeting his guys. Even Arno, as he had learned with Jonathan's trashy cousin Kelli, was occasionally played by girls.

Mickey did a quasi-somersault and landed between Suki and Arno. "Suki," he said, "righteous."

"Another one of my guys from the city."

"Uh-huh. Hey, Arno, got any whiskey?" Arno passed Mickey the flask and he took a swig. "So where's the party tonight?"

Arno and Suki shrugged. Barker's voice came over the microphone: "All right, girls and boys, *buona serra*! And just a friendly reminder: Anyone caught with illegal substances tonight will be flying home tomorrow. The RAs will be doing room checks at midnight, so you have about an hour to do what you have to do before bedtime."

The kids gave a collective groan and then started to stand up.

"Shit, I gotta get back to my group," Mickey said. "See you later."

Arno waved at him exaggeratedly. "Buh-bye." It was about time he got going.

"And *you*," Mickey said, pointing to Suki, "I will definitely be seeing later."

David is to ocean like wet is to blanket

"Hey, have you seen my friend Patch?" David Grobart asked a little redheaded Brit who was standing by the edge of the deck and having a last cigarette before the teachers kicked everyone downstairs. He'd been looking for his friends for half an hour, and if he didn't find them soon he was going to have to go back to his room by himself. Then he'd never find out where the party was.

"Patch *Flood*?" the girl asked incredulously. She flicked her cigarette over the edge and turned to walk away. As she did, she called after him, "Your friend? Yeah, *right*."

That was a new low for David, and already he was having a terrible time. It was just like summer camp, except worse. At least in summer camp there were lots of other guys who sat around awkwardly at night. David had been in good company then. But on the Ocean Term's cruise ship, sailing under a perfect, star-littered Mediterranean sky, David was pretty sure he was the only awkward guy on board.

And to make matters worse, he was kind of drunk. One of the guys in his orientation group had brought a thermos of Irish coffee and they'd all had some of it. In fact, he must have had more than he realized. And then there were the one or two (two or three?) beers he and the guys had had in Patch's room, before evening lecture. As he walked downstairs to the student cabins, he felt increasingly unsteady.

The movement of the water and the lowness of the ceilings only contributed to his disorientation. Back home in New York, he was a basketball player for Potterton. He was six four, and known for occasional bouts of sensitivity. The halls, which were filled with girls in tank tops and their chatter, seemed to be closing in on him. David walked by, catching snippets of conversations. Who so-and-so liked, wasn't so-and-so a bitch, which room they should meet at after room check. He wandered aimlessly for a while, and then he did the same thing he would have done in New York. He headed for Patch's room.

Patch's room was sort of out of the way, and there were fewer and fewer kids the closer he got. As he turned on to his hall, he heard voices, and then he was pretty sure he saw Patch: He was leaning against the wall and pretending to listen to some big guy talk. But he wasn't listening. Even David, in his sorry state, could tell that. He looked bored.

"Hey, Patch," David called. He was so glad to see him that he started to run. As he did, his toe caught in the carpet and he fell flat on his face. Humiliation washed over him. He lay with his head down for a minute, trying to think how he might play this off. As he thought, footsteps came down the hall toward him.

"David . . . ?" he heard Patch say.

Then an older man's voice said, "Sailor, are you . . ." David lifted his eyes and looked straight into the ruddy face of Roger Barker. His fat, saliva-strung mouth was forming the word: "Drunk . . ."

"Uh, Doctor Barker . . . ," Patch was saying. But in order to preserve his dignity, and because he couldn't think of anything else to say right then, David had to admit it.

"Yes, sir," he said meekly.

"Stephanie!!!!!" Barker roared.

Before David knew what was happening, one of the other teachers had appeared and he was being dragged through the halls. They went up and down stairs, and finally, when David had absolutely no idea where they were anymore, they reached a small cabin. It was even smaller than David's cabin, which was small to begin with.

Barker sat him down on the bed. "Sailor," he said again, "let's be serious now. Are you drunk?"

"Yes." David choked out the word. The cute girl from the brochure was standing behind Barker. Apparently, she worked for him now.

"There is no drinking on this ship, sailor. I am forced to call your parents and expel you from the program. Now, what is your full name?"

"David Grobart, sir."

Barker turned off the light and left. David heard the lock click. He lay on his back and tried not to think about his situation, but of course, that was impossible. How absurd that *he* was the one who got into trouble. Arno was probably in some girl's room right now, using a minimum of four contraband substances. Mickey was probably taking a very illegal midnight pleasure dip in the pool. But it was David who had ended up in the hole. And then, of course, there were his parents. The Grobarts were both therapists, and try as they might to "be cool" with everything, David already knew that they would treat his expulsion as a personal blow to their already very fragile psyches.

With these thoughts charging through his brain, David became increasingly pissed off. He worked himself into a fury until, finally, exhausted, he fell into a turbulent sleep. After hours of tossing and turning, the door opened, and Barker turned the lights on.

"Come with me, sailor," he said with gravity.

David followed him up to the deck. His suitcases had been packed and were lined up by the exit ramp. It was early morning, and they were moored in Sicily. Barker handed him his coat.

"Your friend Patch packed your bags for you, because that's just the sort of excellent young man he is," he said. "Now, a car is waiting. It will take you to the airport. Your parents have arranged for a flight to take you back to New York. I'm sorry it had to end this way. I understand you're quite a ballplayer. But I run a tight ship, and there will be no drinking on my watch."

"Thank you," David said, which immediately seemed absurd. He picked up his bags and walked down to the car. He took one last look at the *Ariadne*. Up on the deck, Patch, Arno, Mickey, and Jonathan were watching him sadly. They were waving, and they all looked, David thought—his anger rallying for a moment—a little bit hungover.

This is *exactly* what happens when I can't see my friends

"I can't believe it," I said.

"What," said Arno without looking up at me. He was trying to finish his assignment as quickly as possible so that he could swim a few laps before dinnertime. We were sitting in the *Ariadne*'s computer lab, and I had just gotten an e-mail from David.

"Grobart's back in the city and hanging out with that Rob kid—"

"You mean your stepbrother?" Arno interrupted.

"Yeah. And I think he likes it."

"You already *knew* that. They were practically best-fucking-friends on your stepmom's yacht."

"Yeah, but that's when they had limited options. This is *voluntary*. You're telling me, in the whole of New York City, the only person David wants to hang out with is Euro-Rob?"

Arno shrugged and kept typing. All the Ocean Term students had to read *The Odyssey* and write daily responses to it, and Arno had missed the first one and was really late on this one.

"He sounds okay with being back home, though," I said. "I think."

It had been two days since David got kicked off the boat, and we had all pretty much gotten over the oddness of how the most rule-abiding one of us had literally tripped over drunk in front of our fearless Captain Barker. But I'm the one who keeps us all copasetic as a group, so I felt really guilty that David was alone on the other side of the ocean. With Rob.

Arno paused and looked up at me.

"Remind me which one Calypso is . . . ?"

I rolled my eyes.

For the second time, I quit my e-mail account and reopened it. There was still nothing from Flannery "Flan" Flood. We started going out about a month before I left for my dad's honeymoon. I couldn't really talk to Arno about it, but I was missing her a lot and was feeling pretty anxious about how we'd left things. And worse, I knew I deserved to be feeling the way I did.

I took a break from my e-mail obsession and

checked the trip schedule that we'd been given during orientation. And that's when I realized that we weren't just five days into the trip: We were ten days away from being back in New York. And today was Friday, which meant we were probably missing a lot of parties. Instead, we would have a sailing expedition in Menorca tomorrow, a "Free Day" on Mallorca on Sunday, we'd arrive in Barcelona two days after that, and leave port again the following day. Then there was still Thursday, Friday, and Saturday of little day trips in Spain and Portugal, before it was Sunday again and we could board a plane at Heathrow, bound for home.

Just then, a female voice called to Arno. Girls are always trying to get attention from Arno, and he doesn't give it up a lot—at least, statistically, when you consider how many girls are begging for his attention in the first place—which only makes them want it more. We both looked up. Two girls in flip-flops, boy-short bathing-suit bottoms, and worn tank tops were coming toward us. They looked very casual, like they had been sunning on the deck.

"Hey, Suki . . . ," Arno said, flashing his I-am-dangerously-handsome smile. Arno immediately flipped off the computer, erasing what little work he'd done.

"And Greta," I finished, elbowing him not to be a dick. Arno had met Suki in his orientation group, and Greta was her friend from California. Suki was taller and more outgoing, in a cold way. The first time we met, she looked at me and said, "Oh, that's why they call it a *faux*-hawk. Where I come from we have Mohawks for real," as though she were the punkest ever or something. Greta was quieter, and she came from Santa Cruz, which is a place where Patch and his dad sometimes go to surf. Waves of hennaed hair spilled over Greta's shoulders, and there were knots of friendship bracelets around her pink wrists.

"Hey," Suki said when they reached us. Why did she irritate me so much? Greta waved shyly from behind her. "We were wondering if you guys wanted to be partners with us on that project tomorrow," she said to Arno. The teachers had planned a day of sailing for us the next day, on little sailboats—Ideal 18s. We were supposed to choose our own groups of five to seven people. It would be our first sailing practical.

"Yeah, sure. We needed two more people

anyway," he said with a shrug.

"I suspected," Suki said at the same time as Greta said, "Right on."

"Well, I guess we'll see you in the cafeteria for dinner," I said, hoping to get rid of them.

"Sure," Suki snorted, "if I can gather the strength," and then, laughing, she put her arm around Greta's waist and they glided toward the door.

Arno watched them walk away. Then he picked up his copy of *The Odyssey* and threw it at me for no apparent reason. It bounced off my shoulder and hit the ground.

"Are you going to read that or what?" I asked.

"Nah, I got more important stuff to attend to."

"Whatever." I turned back to my screen and quit and reopened my e-mail so I could see if there was anything from Flan. The e-mail program has a Check for New Mail option, but I'm superstitious about that. I'd rather go for a clean slate.

"Oh, by the way . . ." It was Suki. She'd made it to the door, but she hadn't *quite* made it out. "I saw your friend—Mickey? On the deck? And he said he thought we'd all make a real sweet team."

I'm too nervous to actually digest Ocean Term fare

Arno knocked on my cabin door at 6:25. Weirdly, Arno and I have fallen into the same hanging-out habits we have at home. Back in New York we spend the most time together because we go to the same school, even though we aren't the closest in our crew, and now we were doing the same thing. After the computer lab, he'd gone for a swim, and now he was back at my place.

"Dinnertime, Grandma," he called. I groaned and let him in. In Manhattan we would eat dinner at 10:00, or maybe 8:45. Or maybe we'd skip it entirely and build up an appetite for late-night breakfast at Florent when we're all wasted and absolutely starving. Arno flopped onto my bed and rolled his eyes at me.

"I know," I said. "This sucks."

"It would be fine if they didn't *force* us to go."

He picked up one of the magazines I'd left lying around and began flipping through it.

I gave myself a hard look in the mirror and tried to determine whether my outfit was too much. I was wearing white Ben Sherman jeans and an argyle Paul Stuart sweater.

"Do you think this is, you know, too much?" I asked, catching Arno's eye in the mirror.

"Christ," Arno said, throwing the magazine at my head.

"Fine, let's just go," I said. I pushed my hair a few times, so that it re-formed into a crest down the center of my scalp, and kicked on some flip-flops for casual balance.

All the other students were streaming toward the cafeteria. Girls we sort of knew waved at us, and we waved back. We checked our names on the attendance list that one of the faculty people kept at the door, and got in line.

"Great. This looks like cafeteria food," Arno said. The cafeteria was dishing out your basic lunch-line fare—mashed potatoes, greasy chicken, corn, and greens. You get the idea. We both got grayish burgers, fries, and a Coke, and went to find a table. I looked around for Mickey or Patch, but I couldn't see either of them, so we picked a random, empty table. The room was large, with vaulted ceilings. They'd gone for a sort of faux–prep school feel, with wood paneling and wood picnic benches for tables, in long rows as far as the eye could see. There were wall hangings made from sharks' jaws, that sort of thing.

Next to us was a table of jocklike guys shoveling food in their mouths and all yelling at once. Every one of them was wearing some shade of athletic gray or navy blue, with baseball caps turned at odd angles. There was one girl amongst them, a tall lanky blonde. She looked a little like Flan, and I stared at her for a minute until I realized she was way not as beautiful as Flan.

Then Patch came through the line with Barker, who seemed to be escorting him through the many tables of students. The suppertime din quieted to near silence as they passed, and everyone turned to look. Patch has this effect on people: He's golden and guileless, and sort of hard to pin down, too, and he has that very rare kind of cool that happens only when a person has no idea or intention of being cool in the first place. We watched as Barker cut in the food queue and gestured for one of the caf people to make up their trays.

"We've got to save him," I said.

"I don't want Barker anywhere *near* me," Arno said. "He'd probably kick me out based on smell alone."

"Get over it. Patch needs us."

Arno stood up and started waving. He cupped his hands around his mouth and yelled: "Patch! Patch Flood! I just read this *amazing* passage in *The Odyssey*. Come over, I want to share it with you."

The cafeteria hushed again, and everyone looked in our direction. Patch excused himself from Barker and came over to our table.

"Thanks, man," he said. He and Arno did one of those man hugs where they shook hands and then leaned in to slap each other's backs. "That guy's really dragging on my scene. What's new?"

"I got an e-mail from David," I said.

"Oh, yeah?"

"Yeah, he seems like he's taking it okay. Apparently his dad is writing a crazy letter to Barker about what a repressive program he's running and how bad it is for developing psyches blah-blah-blah . . ."

"Sweet."

I took a sip of my Coke and looked at Patch. I tried to look nonchalant. "Oh, by the way . . . you haven't heard from Flan, have you?"

He opened his mouth to say something, but just then that girl Greta appeared over his shoulder, looking a little lost and confused.

"Hey, guys, you haven't seen Suki, have you?" We all shook our heads. She bit her lip and looked around at all the other tables of kids who were having very involved conversations, like they had all been in the same cliques forever, just like us. "Well . . . do you think I could sit with you guys, then?"

"Sure," Patch said, apparently forgetting entirely about my question. I looked purposefully at Patch, hoping he would remember what we were just talking about. But he just gave me this little smile like "Isn't this fun?" and bit into a chicken leg.

"You, like, hang with Suki all the time at home?" Arno asked.

Greta took a bite of potatoes and shook her head. "Mostly on the weekends. But we go to different schools, in different towns, so during the week I spend time with my boyfriend."

"Oh. Do you hang out with Suki and her boyfriend, then?"

"Suki and Kyle broke up *months* ago," Greta said.

This was getting old, and Patch was obviously not going to talk about Flan anytime soon. I looked distractedly around the room and saw something weird.

"Hey, isn't that Sara-Beth Benny?" I asked. Coming toward us was a very petite-looking girl wearing a Missoni poncho over black knee-length shorts. They were cuffed and a little baggy, and accentuated her gorgeous, if slightly too skinny, calves. Her messy hair was a muddle of dye jobs, and her mascara was smudged a little bit. She had that deer-in-the-headlights quality about her.

"From *Mike's Princesses*?" Greta asked. Sara-Beth Benny had been the child star of this sitcom that was popular when we were kids in which Mike, a single dad and Los Angeles stand-up comic, struggles to raise three daughters. Sara-Beth had been the youngest. She was famously wild now; we saw her around New York at parties sometimes.

The jocks next to us all began to sing the *Mike's Princesses* theme song and laugh. Sara-

Beth looked like she was about to cry.

The blond girl who was not as pretty as Flan said, "Jesus, *eat* something," really loud.

Patch shook his head at us. "Those dudes are assholes," he said. He picked up a roll and lobbed it at them. "Hey, chill out. It's like you've never seen a famous person before or something."

The guys all looked sort of pissed, but it's hard to argue with Patch. Especially when the trip's director so obviously adored him. Arno motioned for Sara-Beth to come over.

She set down her tray—which had three pieces of corn on the cob and a Diet Coke on it— and kissed Arno on both cheeks. I had forgotten until then that they had modeled together a few times.

"They know each other?" Greta whispered to me. I shrugged.

"God, doesn't this place *suck*?" Sara-Beth said as she began furiously blotting the butter off of her corn with napkins. "I'm so glad there are some other civilized people on this lame-ass trip."

"Yeah. I'm surprised you're here, actually," Arno said.

"*Totally*. My parents made me come because

they think I have a *problem*, and they thought this would be a wholesome way for me to spend two weeks. Which it so obviously is not!"

Everybody started talking then, and it looked like we might actually be having a good time. It started feeling like New York a little bit, with lots of shit-talking. I tried not to think about Flan all that much, and fought the urge to run off to the computer lab and check my e-mail again. I mean, SB's cool. At least, she's always a guaranteed good time. And the things she was saying about our Ocean Term classmates were brilliantly cruel to the point where even I thought they were funny. She said something that made everyone laugh pretty hard, and then she tossed a corncob over her shoulder.

"Oh, I almost forgot. I just saw your friend Mickey Pardo on my way here. He was walking in the opposite direction with some Asian chick."

Mickey digs a girl who loves to laugh

Mickey Pardo barreled through the lower levels of the *Ariadne*. He had been pent up in this ship for five days, and he had enough unused adrenaline coursing through his squat body to give a small elephant a heart attack. Right before leaving New York, he had shaved his head in protest of his mother's duplicity (his mother loved his hair), so he currently had the aerodynamic advantage of a cannonball. It made him look tough-hot, if not exactly handsome. He was wearing a wife-beater, Dickies cut off at the knee, and nothing else. Mickey had been labeled as basically crazy, which he basically was. He was picking up speed to take a turn, when all of a sudden he saw Suki Davison and stopped dead in his tracks.

She was wearing a white sack dress with spaghetti straps. It was frayed at the edges and hung mid-thigh. Suki had this kind of hippie-chic thing going for her: long yoga limbs, a smattering of brown freckles across her nose, and a small, bee-stung mouth à la Kate Moss.

She always looked relaxed, and nothing ever seemed to rile her.

"Why, 'ello," he said in an over-the-top British accent. Mickey was thoroughly entertained by the Ocean Term Brit kids and the way they talked. Their accents made the American girls swoon, so Mickey took extra pleasure in mimicking them to their faces.

"Hey *vato* . . . ," Suki said joshingly as she took in Mickey's style.

"Where ya going?"

"To the cafeteria. It's dinnertime, didn't you know?"

Mickey looked at his watchless wrist. "That food sucks."

"Yeah, no shit. Imagine if you were a vegetarian. I haven't been full since we left port."

"Veggie, huh?" Mickey scratched his chin and gave her his scheming look.

"Uh-huh, well . . . I guess I'll see you in there . . . ?"

"Why don't you let me cook you dinner in my cabin?"

"How are you gonna *cook*?"

"Don't you trust me?" Mickey winked and extended his hand.

"They take attendance, you know."

"What are they going to do, kick us off the ship?"

"Maybe. I heard about your friend David."

"That was David. I'm Mickey."

"And besides, Greta's waiting for me."

They stood and stared at each other for a minute, and then both their faces broke out in grins. Mickey grabbed her hand and they went running through the halls.

Mickey's cabin was a mess. He shut the door behind them, then he dashed around picking up pieces of clothing and stuffing them into the closet. When he was done he turned to her and gave a deep bow.

"Ta-da."

"*Very* nice," Suki said, clapping her hands twice in approval.

Mickey spread his blanket on the floor so it became a picnic blanket, and gestured for her to sit. She crossed her legs yoga style and leaned back on her palms. Mickey took a bottle of champagne that he had spirited from Jonathan's stepmom's yacht out from the mini-refrigerator. He held it from the neck and showed it to Suki for her approval.

"I've been saving this," he said, popping the cork.

He poured some into plastic hotel cups and handed her one.

"Cheers," he said, and raised his cup.

"Cheers."

They each took a sip, and then Mickey turned back to the minifridge. He took out a container of crème fraîche, a box of crackers, a small jar of caviar, a little silver knife, and a plate (all, naturally, borrowed from PISS). He began to assemble crackers, each with a dab of caviar and a dab of cream, and arrange them around the plate.

"What's that?"

"It's caviar. Haven't you ever had caviar?"

Suki stuck her tongue out. "I told you, I don't eat meat."

"Not even fish?"

"Not even fish."

"You eat eggs, though, right?"

"Well, yeah, okay."

"Well, this is like eggs from fishes. Except that it's like a hundred bucks an ounce, which isn't really like eggs at all."

She gave him a look.

"Here, I'll try one first," he said. He threw his head back and dropped a cracker into his mouth as though it were a sardine. He chewed quickly, then threw himself back on the floor. *"So . . . good . . ."*

He sat up. Suki was laughing and shaking her head.

"I'm not going to sacrifice my principles for *you*, Mickey Pardo."

"C'mon," Mickey said. He picked up one of the crackers and lifted it toward her mouth. She pulled her head back, but she had this enigmatic smile on her face, so he put it closer to her mouth until she opened and took a bite. After chewing thoughtfully, she said, "Okay, that's pretty good. I'll take another."

So he fed her another. She had one, he had one, and they took a sip of champagne until the plate was empty. Then she took out a pack of cloves.

"Do you mind?"

Mickey shook his head. They lay down on the blanket and watched the ceiling fan as she exhaled perfumey smoke rings.

"That's a cool trick," Mickey said, rolling onto his side so he could look at her. Her hair was spread all around her head like a dark puddle, and her knees were up so that he could see most of her long, pale thighs.

"So, like, what do your parents do?"

"My dad teaches physics at Cal, and my mom owns a yoga studio. Yours?"

"My dad's Ricardo Pardo, the sculptor."

"Yeah, right," she said, and they both half laughed. "I think my friend Greta likes your friend Patch."

"Yeah? I think my friend Arno likes *you*."

"Yeah, I think so, too." Suki rolled over so she was

facing him, took his head between both her hands, and kissed Mickey longer and hotter than he had ever been kissed before.

Arno doesn't care if the ocean is amazing

"Isn't the ocean *amazing*," Suki said the next morning. She was leaning against the ledge of their sailboat and tossing her head back like she was inhaling all the beauty of the day. The gesture made her long hair swish back and forth against her high, flat butt. She put her chin on her shoulder and flashed her bright eyes at Arno, who hadn't been looking at the ocean.

"Totally," he said, looking briefly at the water and then turning back to her. "But not as amazing as you. Natch."

"Not as amazing as *yooouuu*," Mickey parroted from behind them in a mocking tone.

To practice sailing, the students had broken up into small groups and were maneuvering Ideal 18s through the Bay of Fornells. It was an inlet in the north shore of Menorca, one of the Balearic Islands, where the *Ariadne* had docked early that morning. Patch was captaining their boat, along with Stephanie, who was their group's faculty advisor. (Arno wondered briefly if Patch was into her—she was only twenty-three, and hot in a sort of athletic way—and if so, what he, Arno, was missing out on.) Greta, Suki's best friend who didn't talk very much, was sitting next to Jonathan on the other side of the boat. Mickey had been standing at the center of the boat until a few minutes ago, holding on to the mast and doing his best Jack Sparrow impression. He had been talking crazy Mickey talk like that all day. Arno could see where this was going.

Mickey jumped down between them and put an arm around Suki and an arm around Arno. Suki gave him the bright, inviting look she had just been giving Arno.

"Ahoy, m'pretties!" Mickey said in his rogue's accent.

They all stood awkwardly for a minute and stared out at the water. It was deep blue and huge under the cloudless late-afternoon sky. The island rose on either side of them, like two great gray-brown sea monsters. The wind was gently rearranging their hair; it had been a lazy, salty day. Even Arno had to admit to himself that it was *actually* amazing. He pushed away from Mickey and took a look over the side of the boat.

"I bet I could beat you to that beach," Arno said, pulling his T-shirt over his head and revealing his perfect abs. He turned and looked at Mickey, who still had his arm around Suki. In fact, he had lowered it to her hip.

"Which beach? That one . . . ," Mickey said, smiling devilishly and pointing at the beach directly in front of them. It was the side of the bay they had come from, and the one they would soon dock at. Then he turned and pointed somewhere over Arno's shoulder. ". . . Or that one?"

Arno turned to look. He shielded his eyes from the sun, but he couldn't see anything remotely near them in that direction. "There's no *bee* . . ." But before he could get the word out, Mickey was over the side and plowing through the waves toward shore. Suki leaned against the edge and clapped her hands. So Arno had no choice but to kick off his flip-flops and dive over the edge.

The water had looked calm from above, and it was a shock to Arno's system when he realized how choppy the waves actually were. He was a good swimmer, though—or at least, he had been a good swimmer during gym class in Gissing's rooftop pool—and he propelled himself forward with several perfect freestyle strokes. He was getting closer to Mickey, when he made the mistake of thinking about how deep the water was and how far from shore they were. *Oh, shit.*

Mickey was not a great swimmer, but he had a lot of competitive energy. As Arno pushed through the water, trying not to focus on his actual situation, he could see

Mickey thrashing about ahead of him. Before long, they were right next to each other, slapping their way through the water. The shore, inexplicably, kept growing farther and farther away. After several minutes of panicky swimming Arno realized he could overtake Mickey, but he was so freaked out by being alone in an apparently bottomless ocean that he kept steady just a few strokes ahead of him, instead.

When Arno finally thought to look back and see what had happened to the boat, there was nothing there. Just one . . . big . . . ocean. *The tide must be pulling us away*, he thought.

After what seemed like an eternity, they were close enough to the beach to see the bottom. Arno waited until they could practically stand, and then he picked up speed, thrusting his torso through the water. He reached the beach first. He staggered onto it, exhausted, and then collapsed. A few moments later he heard Mickey fall down beside him.

"*Dude,*" Mickey said. He was gasping for air. "That was so stupid."

**If only all this beauty could make me miss
Flan less**

I was out of things to say to Greta. We were sitting on one of the sailboats the program had rented from the locals, watching Patch and our faculty advisor, Stephanie Rayder, steer the boat. Greta kept staring up at Patch, which is what most girls do. Unless of course they're staring at Arno. On the other side of the boat, Mickey and Arno were trying to outdo each other getting the attention of Greta's friend Suki.

I was realizing more and more why I didn't like this girl Suki. She was one of these types who, like, needs the attention of two dudes—minimum—competing for her at all times. And that's really pathetic to watch.

Everything was beautiful—very blue, very Mediterranean, with all the little white boats dotting the bay—but I was ready for the sail to be over. I had been ready for it to be over since before it started. In fact, Arno had very nearly had to carry me off of the *Ariadne* that morning, because what I'd really wanted to do was stay close to the computer lab. As of that morning I hadn't gotten an e-mail from Flan in six days, and even though it shouldn't, it was driving me crazy.

And of course, it was more than your average lovesickness that was eating me. When I said things were going good with Flan before I went on this trip, I was leaving out the last time I saw her . . .

New York between Thanksgiving and New Year's is pretty much all holiday parties, which is fun even though it means talking to a lot of people our parents' age. The hostesses all try and outdo each other with amazing holiday drinks, and it's a good excuse to wear new clothes that might not really work for every day. Usually I meet up with my guys there, get a little boozy, eat some hors d'oeuvres, and head out. But this year Flan and I went to all of those things together, traipsing from one warm, festive event to another.

Then, at some point, I started feeling a little trapped. Like, everybody's parents chatting about how cute we looked together got really tired, you know? And plus, all of my guys were acting single suddenly, and going to after-parties or dive bars late at night, and I didn't feel like I could bring Flan along. I mean, she's in eighth grade. So most nights, I ended up going over to her house, or she came over to mine, and we'd watch movies in our fancy holiday clothes. And pretty soon I started feeling a little domesticated, I guess. And the feeling kept building, and I started acting kind of mean, until finally, at the very end of a very drunken New Year's Eve party, I went back to the Floods' Perry Street town house and pulled Flan aside. I said a lot of things, and then I said that I thought we should "cool it, and just see what happens when I come back from the trip." She ran to her room crying. The next morning I flew to Miami.

I had been writing her all these e-mails from PISS's yacht that sort of avoided that event. And she had been sending me back three-sentence notes like: "Went riding this morning. New York is cold. Say hi to my brother. FF." But now even those had stopped coming.

Sailing around in the Mediterranean, Flan in New York—with her white fur stole and earmuffs—seemed like another planet. And that only increased my remorse and anxiety about having pushed her away.

Our side of the boat went up and then down all of a sudden, and I heard a splash.

"No, *they didn't*!" I heard Stephanie yell from the helm, so I stood up to have a look. Arno's T-shirt was hanging from the other side of the boat, but Arno and Mickey were nowhere in sight. Suki winked at Greta.

Stephanie was trying to turn the boat toward shore. She looked either really pissed, or really scared. Patch, who was standing next to her, said something in her ear and she said something back, and then he jumped down and tried to get the sail up. But just when he got it open the wind changed, and we started moving pretty quickly in the opposite direction.

"Everyone *port side*," Stephanie yelled, and then Patch and Suki scampered over next to Greta and me. Which was a good thing, because I definitely wouldn't have been able to remember which side was port side right then.

"What happened?" I asked Patch.

"I have no idea. I just turned around, and Arno was diving over the side after Mickey."

I shook my head.

"Dare?" he suggested.

"Yeah, yuh think?" I replied, perhaps a little more sarcastically than necessary. Patch brushed the sun-bleached hair off his forehead and gave me that big, gray-eyed look that was three-fourths concern and one-fourth hurt.

"That island is way farther than they realize," he said. Then he jumped back up to help Stephanie.

I had a familiar, sick feeling about this. Especially since I was thinking I had Suki all figured out. My clique has exactly one promise that we've all made to each other, and that's that none of us will ever kiss a girl that one of the others likes. It all started with this girl Molly back in fifth grade. David liked her, and then Arno kissed her, and then David moped and they got in all these fights. So I made us all promise: No more kissing girls that one or the other of us is into. Of course, the promise got broken a few months ago, when Arno kissed David's girlfriend, Amanda Harrison Deutschmann. That one wasn't any easier for me to fix. And now I could feel something similar coming on, except this time, David was halfway around the world.

By the time they got the boat turned around,

we couldn't see Arno and Mickey at all. We agreed that the best thing to do was head back to shore as quickly as possible and try to find them before anybody else did.

As the boat sailed back to the island, Greta, Suki, and I kept a lookout for Mickey and Arno. Nobody said much until we saw the dock. Then Suki turned to me with a half smile, and said:

"Why do your friends do such dumb-ass things?"

From: grobman@hotmail.com
To: jonathanm@gissing.edu

Hey man. How's kicks on the pleasure cruise? Ha ha. Seriously man, why didn't you respond to my last e-mail? New York is really cold and my parents decided not to start a letter-writing campaign against Ocean Term. Apparently a lot of their clients are friends with Barker, and it seemed ill-advised. They're still pretending like they don't care that I got kicked off the trip, but they so obviously do. Whatever. They're just going to have to deal with the fact that their son might be kind of a rebel, and maybe I'm not going to Yale like they did. I've been seeing your mom a lot, though, because Rob's like my only friend now, ha ha. It's sort of weird, it's like your house and family and clothes, except Rob's been dropped into them. Your mom loves him, though, which is funny to watch. He's even talking about staying for spring term and doing an internship with her— apparently he's always been really into interior design. Who knew, right? Oh, I ran into Liza Komansky on the street the other day, she said to say hi to you. Seriously man, write me back this time. I'm bored shitless. See you, David.

Patch's world is always warm

"I still can't *believe* your friends," Stephanie said.

"Yeah, I know. A lot of people feel that way." Patch Flood shook his head and passed her the joint. He added softly: "I think their disappearance almost killed Jonathan."

They were sitting on the beach in Ses Salines, the Menorcan village where the *Ariadne* was moored for the night. The beach was long and shallow—it seemed to run the length of the village, and all along it, tourists spilled out of restaurants and bars and went to put their toes in the gentle waves. Ocean Term was docked here for twenty-four hours so that the students could practice sailing. Tomorrow, they were going to the bigger island nearby, Mallorca, for a day trip and then on to Barcelona. It was almost nine o'clock, but there was still light in the sky. The night felt really good to Patch, and he was glad to have escaped the boat. Ever since Barker had chosen Patch as his favorite student, the days had dragged for him.

Stephanie leaned back on her elbows and said, "Thanks for taking a walk with me. I think I really needed to calm down after this afternoon." When Patch didn't say anything, she added: "After spending the afternoon in a rowboat rescuing your friends, I really appreciate it."

"Yo, no worries," Patch said.

"I mean, when I saw them, I was so happy I could have hugged them! But the whole thing really got me angry, too, you know? I guess that's why I blew up like that."

Patch nodded, but he was looking at all the lights coming on in the little white houses across the bay.

"They could have cost me my job, you know," Stephanie said, a little bit defensively. She was silent for a minute and then she added: "And, of course, if anything had happened to those kids on my watch, I just would never have gotten over it."

Stephanie was a twenty-three-year-old NYU junior who had taken several semesters off already to do Ocean Term. She was short and tan and she kept her curly, dirty blond hair pulled back from her face in a ponytail. She had big breasts, and they stretched the program's motto—*Be a Student of the World*, which was printed on her T-shirt—across her chest in an arc.

"You just seem so much better at this kind of stuff.

Like you enjoy hiking and learning about other cultures, and you're not always looking for the easy out. Like your friend Jonathan seems like he's so concerned about his clothes that he can never really appreciate his surroundings."

She passed the joint back to Patch.

"Yeah, Jonathan's not good at outdoorsy stuff. But he's good at lots of other things."

"You really love Jonathan, huh?"

"He's like the one that holds us all together. Sometimes I don't think it's worth it. But other times, it really makes sense and it makes us all really chill. I don't think I can really explain it."

Stephanie threw herself back into the white sand and sighed deeply. "I just don't know how anybody couldn't *love* this. Isn't it all just so *beautiful?*"

Out in the bay, there were a few boats on midnight fishing trips. Patch wished, in passing, that he was out there. "Yeah," he agreed, releasing a long exhale, "it is."

Someone was coming toward them from the party up the beach. Stephanie grabbed the joint and buried it quickly. She took a little bottle out of her purse, which she sprayed in her mouth and then handed to Patch. Patch couldn't decide whether he should use it or not. The way he'd grown up, the idea of hiding anything seemed sort of alien.

"Don't worry," he whispered to Stephanie, "I think it's Arno."

Sure enough, Arno was walking up the beach. He was wearing linen pants and no shirt. And he wasn't alone.

"Then who's that with him?" Stephanie hissed.

Patch tried to focus his eyes. He wondered for a minute how Stephanie could be so tense, because her pot, well, it was good. The person with Patch was definitely a girl, and she was swigging from a bottle.

"*Suki?!*" Stephanie exclaimed, sounding more irritated than concerned.

Suki and Arno stopped dead in their tracks. Suki put the bottle behind her.

"Hey, guys," Arno said, cocking his chin hello to Patch. They all looked at one another suspiciously for a long minute.

"Well, you kids have a good night," Stephanie said eventually. "Don't forget to be on the boat by midnight. We go to Mallorca first thing tomorrow."

"Okay."

"Sweet dreams," Suki called out, carefully maneuvering the bottle in front of her as she and Arno moved down to the dark part of the beach.

When they were far enough away, Suki turned to Arno and asked, "Is your friend crushing on teacher?"

"Who cares?" Arno said, putting his arms on her hips and pulling her down into the sand on top of him. "What I'm interested in is who you're crushing on."

Suki looked like she hadn't heard him. "It would be a shame, that's all," she said.

Then she turned her face toward Arno and looked at him like she'd never seen him before. She brushed a few strands of hair out of his eyes.

"I should probably tell you that I made out with your friend Mickey last night," she said, sucking in her breath and widening her eyes sweetly.

Arno cocked a confident eyebrow and let out a dismissive little laugh. "I thought so," he said dryly. "Doesn't surprise me."

"I'm always getting myself in these dumb situations." Suki giggled. She almost sounded nervous. "I didn't mean to kiss him, but then I did and . . . *Oh!* I hate myself when I'm dippy like this. Do you . . . hate me?"

"Nah." Arno sat up and dug his toes into the sand. He could tell that Suki was staring at him, and that she wanted to know what he was thinking. He put his hand on her head and played with her hair.

"I don't suppose Mickey mentioned Philippa Frady before he kissed you?"

You can't keep a Pardo down

As usual, the party was on in Cabin 101. It was Mickey Pardo's room and, zero-tolerance policy be damned, the booze was flowing. Everyone seemed like they were having a great time except the host. None of his crew as there, and he sat cross-legged in the corner of the bed wearing a straw hat and swigging from a fifth of Cuervo. The six girls dancing at the center of the room were squealing, and everybody else was chain-smoking and sitting or falling into every available inch of floor space. This was one hell of a fire hazard; it was a miracle it hadn't been broken up yet. Mickey couldn't be bothered, though. When he heard the new The Streets album, he yelled, "Turn it up."

There was a knock at the door and for a minute everyone froze. Then Jonathan came in. Greta was with him.

"What's up?" Mickey said. Jonathan and Greta pushed over to him.

"Mickey, you *hate* Cuervo. What are you doing?"

"Where've *you* been?" He looked up blearily. "Hey, Greta."

"Hey, Mickey."

"Do you know where Suki is?"

Greta shook her head, and her cheeks reddened.

Jonathan threw himself down on the bed next to Mickey. He was fidgeting with his fingernails, which Mickey recognized as an anxious twitch. "I just got an e-mail from David."

Mickey barely registered this. "Oh, yeah? That's nice."

"Yeah . . . He sounded . . . good. And I . . . still haven't heard anything from Flan."

For whatever reason, that made Mickey laugh. "J, why are you tweaked about this? From what I can tell, you backed way out of that before the trip."

"Do you think so?"

"Who's Flan?" Greta asked.

"Nobody," Jonathan said at the same time as Mickey said, "Patch's pwitty wittle sistuh."

"Anyway," Jonathan continued, "I'd just like to . . . hear how she's doing."

"Yeah, okay," Mickey said. He was feeling more lively all of a sudden. "I'm sure you'll . . . hear how she's doing soon."

"Thanks. So, what about David?"

"What about him?"

"You know, because of Rob."

"You stress too much," Mickey said, jumping up and starting to dance with the girls. "He'll be fine. We'll be back in, like, ten days, anyway."

"I just feel like he's trying to take over my life or something," Jonathan said. He picked up the Cuervo, took a swig, and grimaced. He passed it to Greta. She took a deep breath, tossed her head back, and killed the bottle.

"Whoa!" Mickey yelled from between two sun-bleached blondes. "Did you see that? That girl can *drink*."

Just then, Arno came through the door. He killed the radio.

"Yo," he said, "Stephanie's coming. You all gotta get *out* of here."

Suki darted in from behind him and grabbed Greta's hand. She whispered something in her ear, and they disappeared.

"Yo, what are you doing?" Mickey yelled. "This is *my* party."

"Yeah, well, looks like your party's over," Arno said. They glared at each other for a long moment as everyone filed out.

They began to pick up beer cans and cigarette butts

and collect them in a trash bag. The place was starting to look better. Then Mickey said, "I kissed her first."

"Yeah? Well, she's into me now."

"You sure about that?"

"You challenging me?"

Jonathan took a bottle of cologne out of his canvas tote and sprayed the air. Arno, momentarily distracted, gave him a look of disbelief.

"It was a free gift from Barneys," Jonathan said lamely, lowering the spray bottle of Boucheron Homme.

"Whatever."

Mickey twisted the trash bag shut and kicked it under the bed. The cans made a gigantic rattling noise, and that shut Arno up. Mickey crossed his arms across his chest and said, "Challenge."

"Guys," Jonathan said, "can't you remember one simple rule?"

Arno shrugged and looked back at Mickey. "Fuck the old rules. May the best man win."

"I'm all for that," Mickey said. He threw his head back and let out a loud war whoop.

Meanwhile, on the other side of the pond . . .

"Two Jäger shots!" Rob yelled over the whooping and howling of the Bulgarian Bar's Saturday night crowd. The bartender, a petite brunette with a vague whiff of the international about her, nodded impassively and put two shot glasses in front of him. He leaned in against the bar and ran his fingers through his hair. "Make it three. One for me, one for *mi amigo Daveed, y uno también para ti, mi amor.*"

Earlier that evening, as they consumed a dinner of french fries with mayo and grappa at Le Père Pinard, Rob had described the Bulgarian Bar to David. "It is supercool, it is like pure chaos. One of the few places you can experience pure Bacchic chaos in our technocratic society of today," he explained, gesticulating and lighting a new cigarette with his old one. His English vocabulary increased suddenly, as though he were quoting something. David nodded, although this sounded suspiciously like the form of extreme therapy that his father, Sam Grobart, had helped pioneer in the seventies.

It was a cold night, and they had to walk through a slushy pile of snow left over from the storm to get to the entrance. The place was on the second floor of a building on East Canal Street, and the klezmer/punk/dance music was already deafening as they came up the stairs. David was secretly relieved to see how dense and manic the crowd was. He'd been feeling self-conscious about his usual Nikes/jeans/white T-shirt uniform all night. But the atmosphere inside the Bulgarian was riotous enough that David could be pretty sure nobody cared what he was wearing.

David stood fidgeting behind Rob, who was laying it on thick with the bartender.

"Salud!" Rob yelled, elbowing David to pick up his shot. They threw them back. David shook himself back into focus and saw that the bartender was smiling at him mischievously. Before he could think what to do, she leaned across the bar and kissed him full on the mouth. He thought guiltily about Amanda Harrison Deutschmann, his still-sort-of-girlfriend. But then all he could think about was how good kissing somebody new felt. The bartender pulled away and winked at him, and before he knew what he was doing, David leaned over the bar and was kissing her heavily.

When he stepped back, the crowd around him erupted in cheers at the public make-out session. Rob patted him on the back appreciatively. "Next girl's mine, okay?" he whispered to David, sounding like he was half kidding. Then he turned back to the bartender. "Another round, *bella*," he said, waving a twenty in the air. "And two Heinekens."

"Those are on me, boys," she said in a hard-to-place European accent.

They took their drinks, the bartender still smiling coyly at David, and headed to one of the booths in the shadows.

The center of the room was like a high-fashion mosh pit. Skinny Polish girls were being swung around by the jumping, yelling dudes. The music was just about the loudest David had ever heard. They watched for a minute, and then Rob yelled, "C'mon!" and tried to pull him up and onto the dance floor. Before David could say "I don't dance," he was swept up into a very fast, very drunk crowd of people.

Girls started to come up to them from the dance floor. David looked over and saw that Rob was dancing pretty suggestively with some girl he thought he recognized from Potterton. Another girl, slightly round with a shock of bleached blond hair and wearing a much-safety-pinned wife-beater, approached David and put her arms around his waist. She looked up at him and smiled a wide, careless, dark-red-lipstick smile. She didn't move very much, just sort of twitched her hips and kept her eyes down. David tried to follow her rhythm and let go a little bit.

Finally the music stopped while a new deejay set up. The dancing mob dispersed, and David looked around at the room. The walls were paneled with fake wood, and the ceiling was strung with Christmas lights. There were plastic cups and beer bottles all over the floor, and the tracked-in snow was melting into the spilled drinks to make a dirty lake at their feet.

"I'm Caroline," the girl said, looking up, but not taking her arms away from his waist.

"David."

"You want to come over to our table?" she asked. He nodded, and looked around for Rob. *Where'd that dick go off to?* he wondered.

Caroline dragged him to a booth crowded with glam-punk types who managed to look very bored despite the raucous crowd all around them. They squeezed in, and she began introductions: "David, this is Leo, Moira, Rex, Bill, Sandra, and February."

"February?" David's mouth hung open.

"David Grobart," Patch's older sister, February Flood, said, tossing back her spiky hair. "What in the hell are *you* doing here?"

71

Is Arno going soft?

"I don't get it," Patch said. He and Arno were lying on their bellies on deck, watching Suki and a bunch of other girls do sunrise yoga. Suki was executing a perfect dhanurasana. Although Arno hated anything remotely New Age—especially any stay-young-forever fad that his mother fell for—he was thinking that Suki's contortionist pose was kind of pervy-hot. Patch sighed. "I mean, I sort of get it. But she's totally not your type. Why are you and Mickey ripping each other over this girl?"

Arno had really wanted someone to talk to, and he'd thought Patch would be perfect. After leaving Mickey's room in a huff, and spending a lonely night trying to read *The Odyssey*, he was feeling a little alienated from his crew. Suki had mentioned the yoga class as an excuse not to spend the night in his cabin, so around five a.m. a sleepless Arno went to look for Patch. After he realized that Patch wasn't in his cabin, he'd gone to Barker's study and politely interrupted. Barker looked up from his desk, where he had been enjoying a twenty-year-old scotch as Patch sipped orange juice. Patch twisted in his chair and gave Arno a save-me-now face. Arno smiled at Barker, revealing a mouth of dazzling white teeth, and reminded Patch about their dawn jog-around-deck date. The older man nodded approvingly and excused them. Arno had been psyched about his craftiness, and glad to have his friend back from the grown-ups. But he hadn't expected Patch to get all Jonathan on him.

"Dude, she's hot," Arno said.

"Dude, how many hot girls do we know?"

"Dude, she's *different*."

"Do you know what you sound like right now?"

Arno paused, and pushed his hair, which he was wearing in a sort of mod mop these days, out of his eyes. "Look, I know I'm not sounding like myself, but I think all that bullshit between Mickey's dad and my mom might have changed me. I'm really starting to think about how being with a lot of girls is just my way of wasting time. And about, you know, commitment."

Patch was silent.

"I mean, Suki's not like anyone we know in New York. I could have a totally alternative, bohemian thing with her that would be so polar opposite of all those art world lies." Arno was almost convincing himself. He

73

couldn't help adding: "Besides, she would irritate the shit out of my mom."

Then an image of Suki and his mom doing yoga together sprung into his mind, and he shuddered in horror.

The sun was coming up over the water now, and they could see that they were in the port of a new city. Out on the Paseo Maritimo that ran along the bay, shopkeepers were setting up fruit stands. Cathedrals and fortresses of another era rose up behind them. Patch seemed to have drifted off for a moment. When he looked back at Arno, he said, "Listen, all I'm saying is we're on this boat for another week. You'll have a whole lot more fun if you aren't trying to go up against a mad Pardo the whole time. Naw mean?"

Arno nodded. There was nothing he hated more than being told what to do. So he turned to Patch and said, "So what's up with you and that RA chick?"

But as usual Patch wasn't listening. He had a thinking look on his face, and after a few beats, he turned to Arno, as though Arno hadn't just said something, and said, "You know what I like? When I come home after skating around or whatever, and you guys are all just in my house. It makes me feel like that place might actually be home."

Arno's first instinct was to say *You know what you*

sound like? in a sort of mimicking tone. But what came out of his mouth was totally different: "Yeah, sometimes I just feel like we're always going out. It's nice to feel like there's somewhere that is our, you know, home base."

"How about tonight the crew just shows up at my cabin, like we would in New York, and we see what happens?"

They heard a footstep overhead.

"What's the plan?" Suki asked. Before either of them could say anything she knelt down and kissed Arno. It was the sort of gray-area peck that could either be romantic or friendly. She stood up and threw her arms in the air. *"Wooo-hooo,* I feel *so good."*

Arno watched as she reached into her bag—it was one of those sack things you can buy at health food stores—and took out a cigarette. She smoked those hippie clove cigarettes that smell like a Morrocan bazaar. She took two drags, and then slapped her forehead dramatically. "Silly me! I *completely* forgot that I quit smoking these things forever this morning," she said, handing the lit clove to Arno. "I'm such a goose. You'll take care of that for me, won't you? Thanks. I'm going to go shower and stuff, but I'll see you guys at morning meeting at eight thirty, right?"

With that, she skipped off—literally skipped—

across the deck and was gone. The two guys remained on their bellies, watching the city slowly come to life. Arno took a long, meditative drag of the clove. Then he stubbed it out because it tasted absolutely disgusting.

Patch makes teacher's pet look like a dream job

"Good morning, sailors!" Stephanie was standing behind the lectern of the lower-level lecture hall. The rest of the faculty were sitting on the stage, to her left. They were mostly college-age kids like her, and as usual they were a wearing a lot of polar fleece and Gore-Tex. Patch walked down the middle aisle behind Arno, and Arno thought he saw Stephanie wink at Patch. They surveyed the room for a minute and then saw Mickey in the fifth row. He was sitting next to Suki and Greta. Arno cocked his chin in their direction, and Patch followed him over. As they took their seats, Stephanie continued to talk.

"Now, we're going to have a beautiful day trip to Mallorca in just a few hours. But before that, I want to tell you about the survival test. It's the biggest challenge you'll face here at Ocean Term, and it's going to begin tomorrow morning. The survival test will take place over twenty-four hours. You will divide yourself up into 'survival teams,' and each team will earn points based on their creative abilities in the wilderness and on their cohesiveness as a group."

Mickey leaned over and hissed at Arno, "Think that pretty face is going to help you when you're out in the real world?"

Without turning his head, Arno whispered, "I'd hardly consider an Ocean Term survival night the *real world.*"

Patch tried to shush them. Usually he wouldn't have cared—if he'd even noticed, he would have assumed they could handle themselves—but right now he was sort of hoping not to catch any more of Stephanie's attention. He enjoyed her company, but he didn't want the entire student body of Ocean Term thinking that Barker *and* Stephanie were enamored with him.

". . . when I was a student at Ocean Term," Stephanie was saying, "not so long ago, the survival test was one of the most rewarding things I did, so I encourage each and every one of you to do it. But, for those of you who don't feel up to it, we have an alternative written exam. But I really, *really* encourage you to do it. I'm passing around this clipboard. Please sign up in teams of three to five on the first page, or, for those of you who *really can't handle it,* put your name on the second page to take the exam."

Mickey wasn't listening anymore. He hissed, "What,

you scared, pretty boy?"

"Survival challenge? I can take you. Easy," Arno shot back.

They both looked back at the stage. Stephanie had moved to a chalkboard and was drawing a big oval with little cresting waves all around it. "We're very lucky at Ocean Term because several years ago Dr. Barker inherited a small island between Mallorca, where we will be moored today, and Barcelona in mainland Spain. That's where the survival test will take place. So we're going to have a nice relaxing day on Mallorca today, and then tomorrow morning we'll approach Barker Island. You will break into your groups, and travel to the island by dinghy. Once there you will . . ."

Suki leaned over Mickey's armrest. "Are we a group?"

"Hell, yeah," Arno and Mickey replied at once. She smiled and leaned over to whisper something to Greta.

"It's on," Mickey said.

"It most definitely is," Arno replied.

". . . during the survival test, myself and a few other staffers will monitor your progress in several areas. The test will conclude with a group swimming race from the island to the ship. We don't want to tell you any more, but how you work as a group, and how you make use of the tools you're given, is a major part of the scoring. Any ques—"

Just then the door banged open and Jonathan came dashing down the middle aisle. He looked severely freaked. His faux-hawk had gotten much hawkier.

"Jonathan, what happened?" Stephanie asked, her face making an affected concerned-frowning expression.

"The Internet is *broken*," Jonathan said, a little winded. "So, I'm sorry I'm late. But I've been talking with the tech people all morning trying to get it up and running. Everyone should stay calm, but it looks really bad."

Stephanie's face broke out in a relieved smile. "Oh, Jonathan, you're cute. But it really doesn't matter because today we're going to Palma, Mallorca's capital, and tomorrow we go on our survival test. So there won't *be* any Internet."

"Survival *test* . . . ?" Jonathan said, his eyes widening to milky saucers. Patch grabbed him by the elbow and pulled him down into a seat.

"You can take a written test, instead, don't worry, man," Patch said.

"What does *that* mean? I'm not afraid to do survival!" Jonathan said, grabbing the clipboard as it came around and writing himself into a group with Patch and two Brit girls from his orientation group.

Everyone continued to buzz with excited little

whispers. When Stephanie wrapped up the morning's announcements, she told everyone to go back to their rooms and get ready for a free day in Palma de Mallorca.

"Just don't forget your passports," she said. "And remember to be back on the boat by seven thirty. We set sail for Barker Island at eight o'clock."

Maybe Arno isn't on top . . .

Arno went to Jonathan's cabin and let himself in.

"*Dude*, what are you doing?" Arno leaned against the door and crossed his left ankle over his right jauntily. He was pretty sure he'd won Suki the night before—so sure, in fact, that he was feeling a little sorry for Mickey—and he was eager to get her off the boat and have her to himself for a while. "It's our last free day before survival hell, and we're going to miss it because you're doing your hair."

"I was just hoping the tech people would give me a call and let me know that the Internet is up and running before we went ashore," Jonathan said weakly, meeting Arno's eyes in the mirror.

"J, don't be a douche. There're Internet cafés on shore. You can wait a few hours. And besides, remember the New Year's Eve we spent on Ibiza, what was it, three years ago? You loved it. So let's mother-fucking-go."

Jonathan sighed and grabbed his Jack Spade suede

tool bag. "What are *you* bringing?" he asked.

"Um, wallet, passport, sunglasses? I mean, you don't need an *overnight* bag here, J. Oh, and Stephanie left us a memo this morning reminding us to take out whatever plane tickets, travelers checks, etcetera, we might have in our wallets, 'cuz if we lose that stuff, we're fucked."

"Right," Jonathan said as he removed a hefty manila envelope from his bag and set it on the bed. He was wearing a white V-neck, Helmut Lang white cords, and his Gucci loafers; he wasn't exactly going to look like your average American backpacker. He threw his argyle sweater in the bag for good measure.

"Can we go now?" Arno prodded.

They walked up to the deck. Most of the students were already on shore, although there were still a few, dressed for a day of beach and sun, debarking with them. Arno and Jonathan met Mickey and Patch on the dock. Greta and Suki stood with them, wearing big sunglasses and American Apparel cotton short shorts, red for Suki and blue for Greta. Suki's long dark hair hung over her shoulders in two braids.

"So what's the plan?" Jonathan asked glumly.

"Stephanie was saying that the old town is really cool, with castles and cathedrals and things," Patch offered. Pretty much everyone groaned.

Mickey flipped a tropical-design beach towel over his head. "I am all about the beach."

Arno tried to think quickly. If he could come up with another activity that left Mickey at the beach by himself, or better yet, with Greta, then Arno could have Suki all to himself. What came out of his mouth sounded pompous even to him. "That's so *frivolous*," he said. "We should really go into town and try and get some gifts and things. You know, for our moms."

"For your mom?" Suki giggled and winked. "Arno, you're too much."

"Come with me."

Suki bit her lip. "I'd love to, but Greta and I are actually going to the beach," she said, gesturing at their beach bags.

Mickey did a little jig. "You could come with us, I guess, but that would probably feel a little, um, I dunno, frivolous."

"Fine, whatever," Jonathan said. "I'll go with you, Arno. I didn't bring a bathing suit anyway. And we can buy stuff and check our e-mail at the same time."

"Guys, I think I'd rather, um, explore the town," Patch said. "Let's all do our own thing and whatever and then tonight we can meet up for dinner. Cool?"

"Oh," Greta said.

"Fine, great," Jonathan said.

"See ya!" Mickey cackled. Arno watched as he walked off down the bay side promenade, holding hands with Greta and Suki. He cursed himself for making such an amateur's mistake.

Stephanie came up behind them then, wearing her usual jean cutoffs, tight Ocean Term T-shirt, and tossing her head of curls.

"Are we going to go see some gorgeous Catalan architecture or what?" she asked, her big toothy smile spreading all the way across her face. Patch nodded to the guys, and he and Stephanie headed into the warren of streets above the docks.

"Listen," Jonathan said, unfolding a map he'd gotten from somewhere, "if we go up Maritimo, which I *think* is what we're on, like seven blocks or something, then take a right on Calle de San Cristobal, and then if we go, like, two blocks we'll be at the Ciber Tango Café . . ."

But Arno was so furious he wasn't even listening.

Mickey and the girls get a taste of the good life

"Oh . . . *yeah* . . ."

Mickey leaned into his chaise lounge and took a sip of his mojito. He wiggled his toes and brushed the sand off his chest. Next to him, Suki and Greta had arranged themselves on their lounge chairs so as to catch the best sun rays. They had taken the bus to Playa de Palma, just outside the city, where the water was warm and gentle and the beach was wide and sandy. After a few hours of running in and out of the waves, they rented chairs and ordered drinks. All around them, lithe, tanned Spaniards and fat, pink English tourists were drinking and lounging and reading *Hello!* magazine. Mickey had been feeling good. Now he was feeling even better.

"If we had more of *this* over *there*," Suki said, pointing first at the beach below her and then at the *Ariadne*, which they could see docked on the other side of the bay, "this trip would be a whole lot more fun."

"Ew, look at *that*," Greta giggled. She pointed at the large, pale, dimpled rear of a touristy-looking woman walking by them who was wearing a (thankfully) one-piece green bathing suit decorated with mauve flowers.

"American or Brit?" Mickey asked.

"Definitely American," Suki said. "If she's not, next round of drinks is on me."

"Aye, luv!" Mickey called in faux-Cockney. The woman turned to them, looking first confused and then pleased when she saw Mickey Pardo, the Latin fireball, waving at her.

"*Ayyyee, luv,*" she replied, putting a hand on her hip and cracking a thin-lipped smile at him.

"Ohhhh . . . hi," Mickey said, his smile fading and his accent switching back to American. "I thought you were someone else. Sorry!"

They all suppressed giggles until the wide British lady was safely gone, and then they broke out in hooting laughter. When the hilarity subsided, Suki stood up and put her floppy straw hat on.

"Well, I guess it's drinks time. Three mojitos?"

"Yes, please!"

"Thanks, sister." Mickey gently slapped Suki's thigh as she turned to walk up the beach.

When she had disappeared into the palm-fronded shack near the beach's entrance, Greta sighed and relaxed back into the chair.

"The water's so *turquoise*," she said.

"We don't have beaches like these in New Yawk City."

"Yeah, or in my town, either. I mean, we go to the beach all the time because my boyfriend is, like, a surfer. But it's never calm and tranquil like this."

Mickey, who hated calm and tranquil, fought the urge to run down the beach and pants all the European dudes in their idiot Speedos. He took in the air and the sun and the salt air for a few good minutes until that urge passed, and then he turned to Greta with his signature wild-eyed smile.

"So give it to me straight: Is your girl into me, or what the fuck?"

Greta opened her mouth to say something, but quieted when she saw Suki coming up behind him with a tray of drinks. Once she had handed them around and resettled into her chair, an awkward silence descended. Greta took a few obligatory sips of her mojito and then excused herself, saying she wanted to take one last dip before it got too late.

Mickey watched her until she had splashed in and taken a few strokes out to sea, and then he leaned over and began to kiss Suki. She tasted cold, like sugar and rum and ice, and Mickey was feeling good until he realized that he was kissing her way more than she was kissing him. Then she pulled back and bit her lip.

"Listen, Mickey. I like you, and we had a really lovely night the other night, but I think I—"

"Like Arno," Mickey said with a tone of weary disgust.

"Well, yeah, I guess . . . Yeah, I do. But that's not really the point. He told me about Philippa."

"What?!" *That* pissed him off. "She's my *ex*-girlfriend."

"Yeah, I know. And it was hella shady for Arno to tell me. But still, doesn't it seem like you might, just *maybe*, be rebounding?"

Mickey had to sort of acknowledge this to be true. Pretty much all his rambunctious, self-destructive energy right now could be chocked up to his split from Philippa Frady. Making it all even worse was the fact that it had been an amicable, reasonable, tentative breakup—which really wasn't the Pardo style. He was so taken in by Suki's calm logic that he almost ceased being angry at Arno. Then he thought of Philippa and how in love with her he was.

Suki reached out and touched his hand. "I think I'm going to go find Arno, okay?" she said softly, picking up her beach bag. "Could you tell Greta that I'll meet her on board at eight?" She bit her lip again and gave him a pained, apologetic look. "Maybe I'll see you at that party in Patch's cabin tonight. And, Mickey? Sorry."

Mickey watched Suki walk off the beach. She went the wrong direction, and then had to turn around and walk all the way back to the entrance they had come in through. She was adorable, and she was going to find Arno: Arno, who had double-crossed him by bringing up Philippa, the girlfriend Mickey had just begun to not obsess over. Mickey was pretty near boiling point, and he began to the thrash around in his chair. He started sort of wrestling with it, and then all of a sudden, the whole thing collapsed.

As he pushed himself up, a little stunned, from the wreckage of the lounger, he saw Greta O'Grady rising out of the water and coming toward him. And suddenly, it was like she was someone he had never met before.

Patch makes like a hero, again

"Lovely day for a *corrida*, isn't it?" Barker called out, raising his wineglass in Patch's direction. Barker had caught Patch and Stephanie wandering happily around the town and roped them into going to a bullfight with him and the Spanish minister of tourism. The minister of tourism had already told them, at length, how he spent every winter on Mallorca, and also how he and Barker had been backpacking buddies in the sixties. He looked like Barker, too: They both wore gigantic sun hats and rubbed their considerable bellies. The deputy minister of tourism was with him, and he was much younger and more handsome than his boss. They were all lined up on the stone coliseumlike seats of the bull-fighting stadium, and Patch was pleased that at least he was sitting all the way on the end.

Patch nodded in Barker's direction. He didn't really get why any day would be a beautiful day for slaughtering animals, and he didn't really get why they were there. Patch and Stephanie had planned to spend the day exploring backward corners of the city, maybe going for a little surf in the afternoon, and now, somehow they'd ended up with Barker again.

"I'm *so* sorry," she whispered in his ear. She sort of nuzzled at it, too. Patch was feeling restless and kind of irritable. He tried to push her away gently.

"It's cool," he said.

Patch liked spending time with Stephanie—she had been a lot of places, she was down for anything, she was pretty physical, and those were all things people said about Patch. Plus, he usually went out with stunning, haughty women who were always complicated, and Stephanie was just fun and not like that.

She made a little pouting face and went back to chatting with the minister of tourism and his deputy.

The sixth and final fight was about to take place, and Patch was ready for it to be over. He'd already watched five bulls get killed in roughly the same way, and the whole thing seemed pretty Medieval to him. The fighters themselves teased the bulls and then hid behind these big protective fences, and they never really got close to them until after a guy on a horse, with a lot of armor on, came out and stabbed the bull in the back twice. This was about to happen again.

Down the row, the minister of tourism was describing the beautiful dance of death that they were watching, and Stephanie kept going "Uh-huh, uh-huh," and "Wow." Patch couldn't listen anymore, so he let his eyes drift across the crowd. Then he heard some familiar voices.

"Oh, you're looking for Jonathan? I just saw him, like, come with me," a girl was saying. "Do you have any cigarettes? Everybody here is smoking, and even though I really *shouldn't*, I really want one."

"Nope, sorry," a guy's voice said. "I'll still take a Jonathan, though." That was definitely Mickey.

Patch looked down and saw Sara-Beth Benny coming out from the arcades and into the seating area. She was carrying two beers in plastic cups. Behind her were Mickey, and Suki's friend Greta. Patch couldn't help noticing that Greta was sunburned. He wanted to wave at them and call them over, but when he saw the beer he realized that it would be best to try to keep them away from Barker.

"I just saw them," Sara-Beth was saying. "Where is he? You can come sit with us, too, of course. I'm with Loki. He's an RA, so don't tell anyone!"

"Thanks, that's cool, but we just need to find Jonathan," Mickey said, sounding a little impatient, the way he would if he were talking to a drunk person. "You should probably think about getting back to the boat, too—it's getting sort of late."

Sara-Beth just giggled. They had gotten to the edge of the seats, right above the bullfighters, and she was craning her neck around, apparently trying to locate Jonathan. Patch doubted he was there—Jonathan would never go for something like this—but he couldn't say anything, of course, because it would call attention to Sara-Beth and her beers. Her eyes were scanning across the crowd, and then they fell on Patch and Stephanie's group. Her eyes got very wide and she jerked backward awkwardly. She hit the guardrail—which was, rather frighteningly, only about a foot and a half high—and flipped over it onto the bullfighting field.

Everyone in the stadium stood up and let out a collective gasp.

"Oh, my God," Stephanie cried out, "that's Sara-Beth!"

"A very special student, an American television star," Barker was saying as if to, absurdly, fill in the minister of tourism.

"Ohhh . . . these situations make me feel awful," the minister replied confidentially, his voice quavering.

"Do something!" Stephanie shrieked as she grabbed Patch's arm.

Patch hurried through the stunned crowd and took a look over the edge. All the bullfighters, as well as the bull, were on the other side of the arena. But the bull had sensed the crowd's excitement and was moving curiously in Sara-Beth's direction. He also seemed to still be angry about the wound he had suffered. There was steam coming out of his nostrils.

Sara-Beth had fallen just below Patch, and she was dragging herself out into the arena and holding on to her ankle like she'd sprained it.

The crowd seemed to be in a state of suspended animation, with their breath held and their hands over their mouths. Patch looked at Mickey, who didn't really look like he was aware of the danger. "Holy shit," Mickey said.

Patch turned back to the edge and leaped over it. He landed standing in the dusty arena, and pain shot up through his feet. He was okay, though, and he hurried forward to where Sara-Beth was whimpering in the dirt. He scooped her up and was relieved to discover that she was virtually weightless, like a bag of leaves. The whole stadium let out its breath.

That was when he looked up, and saw the bull, still angry as hell, charging toward him. A whoop of encouragement went up through the crowd. He ran back to the edge and lifted Sara-Beth up toward Mickey and Greta, who grabbed her by the hands and pulled her to safety. Patch turned and saw that it was too late for him: The bull was charging at him, and he was really, really close this time.

Patch dodged to the left, and the bull nearly ran into the wall. Then he twisted his huge, shiny black body around and came back at Patch. The smell of sweat and blood mingling in the dust was overwhelming. Patch dodged right, and the bull missed again. But when he had turned himself around, and again faced Patch, he became confused. Patch sank down on his knees and looked calmly up into the eyes of the bull.

The bull pawed the dirt for a moment and snorted. The crowd was completely silent, and they watched in fear as the bull faced Patch down. But then, incredibly, the bull kneeled into the dirt, too. Patch approached it and reached out to stroke its head gently, and the crowd, seeing this, broke out in a cheer.

Patch rose and led the bull back toward the bull trainer's area on the side of the arena. Once the bull was safely put away, the crowd rushed onto the field and lifted Patch up. They cheered for him and passed him around on their hands. Eventually, he reached the side of the stadium where he had last seen his friends. Mickey was keeping an eye out, and when he saw Patch he grabbed his hands and pulled him away from his admirers.

Patch was instantly surrounded by Mickey, Greta,

Barker, and the others. Stephanie was holding Sara-Beth in her arms. She looked miniature next to Stephanie, who wasn't large herself.

"That's the kind of thing I thought only *I* would ever do," Mickey said, slapping Patch's back. He was obviously impressed.

"You saved me!" Sara-Beth said. "Thank you so much, Jonathan! I promise my agents and managers will make it up to you."

"That's Patch," everyone said.

"Oh," Sara-Beth said with a giggle, "thank you, Patch."

"Well, Patch, my boy," Barker said, "it looks like you've saved the day again."

Patch smiled shyly. He was relieved that Sara-Beth was okay, and that the bull hadn't been killed.

"This is the best student I've ever had," Barker was telling the minister of tourism. "Well, since Stephanie, at any rate."

"You must come stay at my official residence in Madrid . . . ," the minister of tourism was saying

"You will judge the survival test tomorrow . . ."

"We will name a suite in my hotel after you . . ."

"Perhaps you could give your own evening lecture . . ."

Below them, the crowd continued celebrating

without seeming to notice that it had lost its hero. The sun had begun to go down, and soon enough they had to return to the *Ariadne*. They slipped out of the stadium, trying to avoid notice. Barker and the minister went arm in arm, Mickey and Patch carried Sara-Beth, and Stephanie and Greta followed close behind, their faces creased with admiration.

As usual, I'm fashionably late

"Shit, shit, shit!" I put my face into my hands and tried to inhale a normal breath. A few of the vaguely punkish-looking Spanish people around me turned and smirked, and then turned back to their computers. I had been sitting in the Internet café for hours, checking and rechecking my e-mail. There was only one new message in my in-box, from santananumerouno@yahoo.com, which was an e-mail address I didn't recognize. I didn't feel like I could handle any bad news right then, so I decided not to open it. I quit and logged back on to my e-mail account, but there was still nothing from Flan. To distract myself in between, I looked halfheartedly at shoes on the Marc Jacobs website that I thought would look cute on her. I should have taken this as a sign of how deep an obsession this was becoming: I wasn't even thinking about clothes for me.

Arno must have left at some point, but I'd

missed it.

Also, I was feeling a little crazed. I'd had about four espressos, so that the guy behind the counter wouldn't think I was a freeloader, and the caffeine had hijacked my bloodstream.

Eventually I couldn't take the stares anymore, so I collected my stuff and went up to the counter. On my way, I decided that the best thing to do would be to call Flan at home; when I heard her voice, I was sure everything would come magically together.

"*Bueno,*" the guy behind the counter said curtly.

"*Cuanto?*" I asked.

A little machine printed out a bill, and he put it in front of me. Incredibly, it seemed that I had been there for four hours and thirty-two minutes, and I owed four euros for Internet time (which seemed actually sort of cheap) and sixteen euros for the coffee (which seemed absurdly expensive). I reached into my bag for my wallet, and the warm comfort of my dad's AmEx. But when I opened it, I saw that neither the AmEx nor any of my other credit cards were in there. For a minute I panicked, thinking I had been robbed, but then I remembered that I had put all my credit cards in an envelope with my plane tickets and traveler's checks (which my mother had insisted I buy, even though they're basically obsolete since European ATMs take American cards now).

Shit.

I had an American twenty and five euros. I held my wallet out to the guy, so as to illustrate my situation. He stared back impassively. I tried to pull out the twenty, but my hands were so jittery that I fumbled the wallet. It leaped out of my hands like a slippery fish, and I had to kneel on the ground to pick the wallet and the bill up. When I stood, I noticed a big black smudge on the knee of my white Helmut Lang jeans. I tried not to flip about that, and pushed the twenty at the counter guy.

"Not the same!" he said, looking obviously disgusted with me.

"Can't you change it or something?" I was realizing that I really had to pee.

The guy took the twenty and dangled it in front of my nose. He yelled, "No good to me!"

What would you have done, in my Gucci loafers? Though I felt totally bad about it, I turned on my heel and ran. I ran and ran and ran until I had safely lost myself in a crowd.

Outside, it was still the ripe part of the after-noon. I turned off whatever street I was on and ran through the little winding streets, past old, crumbly buildings and cathedrals and beggar women in black until I reached another populated, bustling main drag. I started walking at a normal pace, scanning for a pay phone. Then I remembered that I didn't have my credit card, so there was no way for me to call the States. I walked glumly for several blocks, not caring where I was headed.

I was feeling really cut off, really powerless. And as I walked through the crowds of screaming and laughing vacationers, this feeling of alone-ness intensified. I was beginning to think that maybe I had fucked up so badly with Flan that I would never be able to make it better, and that thought just made me feel way more desperate.

Since I couldn't go back to the Internet café, I figured I'd just go back to the ship. This day was blown to hell anyway. But maybe they'd have fixed the Internet? I walked down whatever street I was on, which seemed to be going toward the docks. That's when I saw it.

Prada. Thank the Lord, there was a Prada store in Mallorca.

I think I remembered reading about this in *Black Book*, how this hot young architect, Rafik Merleau, had designed another highly postmodern Prada store in Spain somewhere. I went into the temple and soon found myself lost in its space-age corridors. Of course, there was fabulous clothing at every turn. I was totally consumed by touching the fabrics and picturing myself in different outfits, although I didn't let myself try anything on because I didn't have my credit cards, and if something fit really, really well, and I couldn't buy it, that would basically be torture.

If my life were a movie, this is where the camera would zoom in on a clock with hands moving around the face at hyperspeed. What I'm saying is: I lost myself in there.

When I came out I felt much calmer, and the air was cooler and smelled of the sea. In my new, chill state of mind I realized what I should have realized hours ago: I could call Flan collect! Her parents wouldn't even notice the charge on their bill, since the Floods are fabulously wealthy and also a little bit out of it. I would just tell Flan how sorry I was, and how much I'd been yearning for her, and this whole nightmare would be over. It was so simple, I wanted to cry.

I found a pay phone, and after a few foiled attempts at dialing out of the country, I got an operator who spoke English (heavily accented English, but English all the same) and he agreed to put me through to the Floods. The phone rang a few times, and then someone picked up. The operator said that he had a collect call from Spain, and then it sounded like he was talking to himself. It sounded like he was telling himself that he didn't want to collect any calls. For a minute I thought I might be going crazy, and then I realized I wasn't going crazy. I was listening to the operator talk to Rob, the stepbrother who was invading my life.

"Will you accept the charges?" the operator asked again.

"Charges? But, Officer, I haven't done anything!" Rob burst out laughing. His English was only marginally less accented than the operator's. It sounded like there were people laughing with him, and they sounded like girls. Could that be . . . my sweet little Flan?

"No, *collect* charges!" The operator continued.

"No collect charges!" Rob parroted. He

repeated himself a few times, like a chant.

For a minute, the fact that Rob would answer the Floods' phone seemed very normal, but then I realized that it only *seemed* normal because it was *my* life. Except with Rob where I should be. First Rob had tried to take over my home, and now he was going for my girl. Why else would he be at Flan's house at—I looked at my Tiffany watch and added six hours to account for the time difference—*two in the morning!* I mean, that was pretty hard to misinterpret.

I slammed the phone down and realized that I was gripping it so hard my knuckles had turned white. Rubbing them distractedly, I left the kiosk.

After taking a few steps, not knowing where I should go, I was stopped by a thought of a very different nature. This was when I started doing the backward calculation: If it was two o'clock in New York, it was . . . eight o'clock here. What was it, seven thirty that we were supposed to be back on board? For the second time that day, I began to run for my life.

As I ran, my head filled with dire thoughts of Flan. Rob was moving in on her, and who could blame him? And by being such a shithead to her before I left, I had basically made the whole thing happen. I felt like someone had taken out my heart and dropped it in the ocean and it was just going down, down, where nobody would ever find it.

Closer to the docks, there was a sort of festival atmosphere: What looked like Christmas lights were strung from all the trees and lampposts, and people walked lazily along the sidewalks. There was music from street musicians, and various performers, just like the ones in front of the Met on Fifth Avenue, were standing around in their weird poses. There was a man painted gold and holding perfectly still. I rushed by him. Then I saw a man dressed as a savage. He was wearing twigs around his head and a loincloth, and his whole body was painted with elaborate designs, like he had a full body tribal tattoo. A crowd was gathered around him, and he looked, well, savage. I pushed through the crowd, since there was no getting around it, and when I reached the center of it, you'll never guess who I saw.

Suki. And not only was she yelling, she was wearing a ridiculous floppy hat that made her look like a middle-aged gardener.

"This is just the sort of representation that keeps civilization in the dark ages!" she was shouting and pointing at the loincloth dude. Then she began making bunny quotes with her fingers: "This is how 'white people' picture the 'third world,' as full of 'savages,' who are 'the other'! Well, I am not going to stand for this." She turned to the crowd and began pumping her fists in the air. *"No le page! No le page el Conquistador!"*

I stepped up to her and took her by the arm.

"Jonathan, thank God you're here! This man isn't even Spanish, he's an *American*, and he's exploiting these people's stereotypes for profit! I mean, *no wonder* the rest of the world *hates* us. Can you blame them?"

I smiled apologetically at the bemused crowd, and whispered, "Do you know what time it is?"

"I don't *own* a watch."

I lifted my wrist so she could check out mine.

"Holy shit."

"Let's get out of here."

Suki grabbed me by the hand and we pushed through the crowd and went running through the streets. We darted through mobs of people, sidewalk cafés, and traffic, across the big thoroughfare and back into the little stone streets near the water. It was very quiet there, and our heavy breaths and the smacking noises our shoes made filled the alleyways. The streets sloped downward, and we built momentum as we hurtled toward the docks. All of a sudden we came out of the old town and onto the Maritimo. We were standing in exactly the place we had parted that morning. I got a heavy dose of that sick, sinking feeling when I saw the *Ariadne*, lit up and glowing like it was the warmest place on earth, gliding across the water and out of the bay. I turned to Suki, and we looked at each other with faces of horror and despair.

Weirdly, we were still holding hands.

Patch could use a little saving, too

The mood in Barker's study that evening was festive, although for the last half hour or so Patch had been finding it increasingly difficult to appear attentive. The minister of tourism had agreed to accompany them to Barcelona, so that he could witness and help judge the survival test, and he had been enjoying himself as much as possible. He brought his deputy along, too. With the minister on board, Barker had insisted that Stephanie have dinner in his study, and she had begged Patch to come along. They had worked their way through five courses and were now facing down a tremendous cheese plate and full tumblers of Armagnac. It was all sitting a little heavy with Patch.

"*Salud*, my darlings," Barker said, in what may have been the tenth toast of the evening.

"*Salud.*"

"To this heroic day."

"To our hero."

"Uh . . . thanks."

"To the Spanish people."

"Quite."

They all drank.

"Well, my boy, you must tell us about your plans," the minister said to Patch.

"Um, plans?"

"Yes, *por supuesto*. Plans. Plans for the glorious life ahead of you!"

"Oh." Patch brushed away his overgrown hair behind his ears. "Yeah, I guess I don't really do things that way, you know? Like, I take things as they come, sort of."

There was an uncomfortable silence, and then a smile broke across Barker's face. "Bravo! Spoken like a true sailor," he said.

Everyone murmured happily. Then there was a timid knock at the door.

"See who it is," Barker told Stephanie.

Stephanie went to the door and began speaking quietly to someone. Patch turned hopefully to the door and saw Greta, with her mass of red hair and her redder, sunburned cheeks, staring shyly into the study. She waved.

"Um, sorry to interrupt, sir," she began, "but we're having a study group for the survival test tomorrow? And it's really not much of a group if we don't have

Patch to lead us."

There was silence, and for a moment Patch feared that Greta would shrink away and leave him here to be force-fed rich food and stiff booze till dawn. But she took a deep breath and stepped a little farther into the study.

"Could I, um, borrow him? Please, sir . . . Pretty please?"

The minister's deputy yawned, and the minister himself followed suit.

"It *is* getting late," Barker admitted. "Yes, of course. If my boy is willing. But I must advise you, dear, the best preparation is a good sleep, so don't cram for *too* long. And, Patch?"

"Yes, sir."

"You'll need your rest to judge the contest tomorrow."

"Thanks, Doc. Nice to, um, meet you guys. Night. Night, Steph."

"Good night."

"Nighty-night."

"Bye."

"It was a pleasure."

"Buenas noches."

"Sweet dreams . . . ," Stephanie called, a little too feelingly, down the hall.

When they rounded a corner, Greta looked at Patch. Her face was all buttoned up with holding smiles in.

"Thanks, man. I was dying in there."

"Hey, no problem They looked like real bores. Fancy, though, huh?"

"Yeah, I guess. If you're into that."

Greta was blushing through her sunburn. "I didn't mean I was—"

"How'd you get so burned?" Patch interrupted softly.

"Oh, I just . . . I was at the beach, and we had a couple drinks and I wasn't paying attention and my skin's so fair, you know?"

Patch nodded thoughtfully. "Ouch. I have some aloe in my room. Do you want to come over and get some? Your skin looks like it could use it."

"Oh, yeah, I would love to, I mean if it's okay and everything I would really, really . . . ."

"Cool."

Greta stopped walking and put her hands over her face. "Oh, wait, shit, no we can't." She took a deep breath. "Something really bad happened. That's why I came for you."

"What?"

"Well . . . have you seen your friend Jonathan since we got back from Mallorca?"

"Um, no. But I've been with Barker the whole time, so . . ."

"Yeah, nobody else has seen him, either. When we were at the beach we lost track of time, and then Suki went off to find Arno by herself. That's when we went to find Jonathan, but then we found you instead and that whole thing happened. When we got back to the boat, and Mickey and I were crossing our names off the attendance sheet, we noticed that Jonathan and Suki had both forgotten to cross theirs off. So we did it for them, thinking they were probably just flustered. But after a couple hours, I hadn't heard from Suki, so I went to talk to Arno and see if maybe she was with him. But he said she never found him, and that he'd come back to the ship without Jonathan. Mickey hasn't seen either of them, either."

Patch took this in.

"So . . . I'm really worried that maybe they lost track of time and aren't on the boat."

"That's so not a thing that J would do."

"Yeah, Suki neither. But Jonathan *was* really weird this morning. And when Suki left the beach it was already really late, and she was looking for Arno in a big city. And she doesn't wear a watch."

"You've looked everywhere?"

"Uh-huh."

Patch brooded for a moment, which was not an activity he had a lot of experience with. "Listen, just don't tell Barker."

"I'm not sure . . ."

"Trust me. Right now I've got to go to my cabin. I think I was supposed to meet my guys there, and this is going to be sort of a crisis because Jonathan's usually the one who . . . It's just going to be weird."

"Okay."

"Thanks for telling me."

"Sure."

Patch started off toward his cabin, but then he thought of something and turned back to Greta.

"Hey, you all right?"

Greta nodded, although she didn't look so sure of it.

"I'm sorry. Your friend's lost, too. Why don't you come with me? First, we're going to make extra-sure they're not on this boat. Then we'll get you some aloe. And then we'll figure out what to do. You in?"

He put a comforting arm around her, and she put her face into his shoulder. And that was how they began the search for their lost friends.

Arno tries to be bigger than that

"She said that?" Arno smiled to himself. Mickey had just told him about his conversation with Suki on the beach. It was gratifying that she had chosen him, although it sort of made the whole prospect a little less interesting.

"Yeah, big shocker," Mickey said. He swigged from his beer.

They'd come to Patch's cabin separately, and it was already filled with people. They'd hung in opposite corners of the room for a while, but pretty soon they were both irritated that all these kids were just hanging out and partying in their friend's room when he wasn't even there.

They'd begun by circling each other warily, and spoke in terse, sarcastic sentences. Then Mickey bitterly related the story of the beach. Arno, feeling remorseful, had stolen them beers from some kids who were already too drunk to notice.

"Hey, man, I'm sorry about the Philippa slip," Arno offered.

Mickey narrowed his eyes at him and took a swig from the beer. "Yeah, that was low. But I guess I didn't like Suki all that much, 'cuz right now, I don't be giving a shit." He cocked his chin toward Patch's wide, soft-looking bed, where a group of girls were sitting and looking out the porthole. There was a great deal of oohing and ahhing, since none of the other cabins had portholes. Then two of the girls started making out.

"Where the fuck is Patch? This is so typical," Arno said without taking his eyes off the girls. They watched for a long moment. But then one of the girls got up and started looking through CDs, and the other fixed her bra and went off the bathroom as though nothing had happened.

"Dude, this room is so much better than mine."

"Word. I mean, is that redwood?"

"I think the paneling in mine is plastic."

"Totally," Arno said, feeling weirdly optimistic about everything all of a sudden. He took out his pack of cloves, thought about smoking one, and then tossed the box over his shoulder. "So you think Jonathan's really lost?"

"Nah. He's probably in the computer lab."

They both laughed and swigged their beers.

The Faint was blasting from Patch's stereo, and the dancing was getting a little bit out of control. Someone started to slam around in the center of the room, and the crowd expanded outward as a few people lost their balance. A big reddish guy fell into Mickey and Arno. Arno thought he might have recognized him from the cafeteria the other night—the red guy had been sitting next to a girl who kind of looked like Patch's little sister, Flan. He had to be at least 240, and curly red hair peeped from under his backward baseball cap. His face was ruddy, too.

"Yo," he said, righting himself and looking pissed off. His eyelids were low, and his mouth sort of snarled up. It was almost like they could see the beer fizzing in his brain.

Mickey and Arno stared at him impassively. His grimace faded into a slightly jolly smile.

"Hmmm . . . do I, um, know you guys?"

Arno arched one of his perfect black eyebrows. It was his signature look—equal parts crazy, reserved, and disgusted—and he turned it on full-wattage now.

"Yeah, yeah, I *know* I know you guys."

Mickey looked at Arno. He nodded ever so slightly.

"Del Berend, from Wichita, Kansas. You guys ever been there?"

They shook their heads.

"I know I know you guys." He furrowed his brow. "Maybe our dads know each other? My dad's a big-shot real estate developer: Sammy Berend? Berend Estates? Maybe you've seen the ads on TV?"

"We're from New York, so . . ."

"New York, huh . . . ?"

Mickey and Arno waited until the light started to come on, and then Mickey suggested innocently: "Maybe he saw the magazine story . . . ?"

Del nodded slowly.

"Vanity Fair?" Arno suggested

"There was a small story in the *Times*," Mickey reminded him.

"*Us Weekly*, of course. That's where most of the pictures were," Arno said, like *Duh.*

Del was nodding more vigorously now. He slapped his forehead. "Of course . . ."

"Yes."

"You guys are . . . You guys are . . ."

Arno sighed deeply and hung his head. "Bill Clinton's fraternal twin love children with an Argentine heiress."

"Ignacio— " Mickey said.

"And Luis Ribera y Clinton," Arno finished.

Del looked like he was about to burst. Again, he slapped his forehead. "Incredible! So what was it like being hid away all this time? Do you guys have Secret Service detail? Are they *on board*?" he asked, whispering the last two words.

A couple other kids were listening in now.

"Does Hillary hate you?"

"Is it true that you grew up in the slums of Mexico City?"

"Come on, no way. You guys are so gullible . . . ," This from a girl, of course.

"He *does* kind of look like Clinton."

"What!?" Arno, who had a perfectly sculptured nose, said. A look of confusion had come over Del, and it looked like it might soon morph into the grimace again. Arno giggled. Mickey elbowed him.

Just then the door banged open, and a girl's voice yelled, "Everybody *out!*"

The crowd scrambled around, although nobody really seemed to actually leave the room. As the crowd rearranged itself, Arno saw that the voice belonged to Sara-Beth Benny. She was standing in the doorway with her arms thrown up, like a gymnast, and her head tilted forward, like a rock star. Her hair was somewhat messed, and she was wearing a clingy black wraparound dress that looked expensive, and tall black leather boots that looked even more expensive. She swayed a little bit on the stiletto heels of her boots, then dropped one arm. The other arm still pointed to the ceiling.

"I said, *out!*"

"Uh-oh," said Mickey, "she's wasted."

"Plastered."

"Blotto."

The CD changed just then, and an old Cars song came on. Sara-Beth perked up immediately. She started twitching her hips to the beat and stomping her heels.

"Wait, you all can stay. I *love* this song! Wooooooooo! Let the good times roll! Who's got some coke!?"

"Oh, God."

Everyone seemed to calm down and return to dancing or smoking or squealing or whatever they had been doing before the interruption. Even Del was back on the dance floor.

"She's about to lose it," Mickey said.

"I think she might have already lost it."

"Somebody's got to get her out of here."

Arno sighed heavily. "Fine. I'll do it."

"Great."

"Why don't you work on getting most of these losers out of here. When I come back, we can have the kind of party we like."

"Right. And, Arno?"

"Yeah?"

"I hope you never do anything that freaking low again."

They gave each other an awkward, appreciative nod,

and then Arno went over to where Sara-Beth was riding on the shoulders of one of Del's friends, pulled her down, and carried her out of the room.

I like to maintain a certain level of lifestyle no matter what

"This place looks like it might be all right . . . ," I said. We were standing in front of one of the big grand hotels that faced the Paseo Maritimo. It was called the Miramar. You could just tell from looking at it that the sheets were all four hundred thread count, the room service was excellent, and that terry cloth bathrobes came with every room.

"I don't know . . . ," Suki said to me. We had been walking around in mild shock for an hour or so, and neither of us looked our best. Her braids were coming undone, and she was still wearing those American Apparel short shorts and flip-flops and, now that it was a little bit cold, she was wearing my Hugo Boss sweater, and none of it really went together. My hair was falling down, too, and I was pretty sure I had pit stains, even though I didn't have the heart to look.

We had finally decided that we weren't going to figure out what to do about being stuck on Mallorca without our ship, not tonight, anyway, and that we should probably just get a place to sleep and rest. I had explained about my wallet, and had promised Suki—who had a Visa card and about sixty euros—that if she paid for the hotel tonight I would call my mom tomorrow and get her to wire money and that would pay for a way to get us out of here.

"Come on. I mean, we're *here*. And it's late. If we don't act now, we might not be able to even get a room."

Suki nodded, and we walked in through the big, glass sliding doors.

The inside was very Iberian-opulent, with red velvet couches and heavy chandeliers and gold leaf everywhere. Ravel's *Bolero* was playing in the background. We could see a few well-dressed people loitering at the bar on the mezzanine. In the corner, behind a huge dark-stained welcome counter, was an officious-looking concierge.

"*Bueno,*" he said, looking us up and down.

"*Buenas noches,*" Suki said. I was relieved she'd gone ahead and done the talking. Her accent was way better than mine. "*Queremos*

123

una habitación para dos personas, por favor."

The concierge rattled off something in really fast Spanish that I didn't catch. Suki said something like: *"Hay algo más barato, señor?"*

The concierge rattled some more rapid-fire Spanish.

Suki leaned toward me and whispered, "Jonathan, their cheapest room is 250 euros a night."

That sounded about right to me. I nodded at her and said, "Can't you just put it on your card?"

"It's like a debit card, you know, linked to my checking account. I'm not sure how much is in there, but I think it's probably around sixty dollars. Besides, shouldn't we try and save as much money as possible?"

The concierge was sneering at us.

Things looked to be going south here, so I stepped forward. Who knew? Maybe he had heard of Penelope Isquierdo Santana Sutwilley, and maybe, just maybe, dropping her name would be better than a credit card. Maybe he would just let us stay, and I could pay with wired money tomorrow. But when I heard the word *"senior"* come out in my flat, American accent, I knew this wasn't going to work.

"*Señor,*" he said with a corrective accent. "May I to suggest to you the hostel? It is perhaps more in your price range."

He plucked a tourist map from the brochures on the counter and fanned it out in front of his. With a pen, he marked an X on the map.

"We are here," he said, and then dragged the pen through the streets up higher into the city. "The hostel is here. *Bueno*, you can take this," he said, folding the map and passing it icily to me.

"Thank you," I said, feeling more like a teen-ager than pretty much ever. Suki and I turned and hurried out of the Hotel Miramar as fast as possible without actually running.

Neither of us could think of anything to say, so we kept quiet and followed the map. It took us up into the old town—through the winding streets that I'd run through earlier that day. We could see warm windows up above, and the laughing and general noise of people having a good time at night. I was breathing in big, wistful breaths of Spanish air when Suki said:

"So *that* was a great idea."

"What does *that* mean? Forgive me, but I think we could both use a good shower and a comfortable bed."

"Oh, yeah? Listen, Jonathan, you and I are stuck together for at least a couple days. So you'd better get used to the fact that I don't live the way you do."

I didn't even know what to say to that, so we just didn't talk for a while. That was, of course, how we got lost. All of a sudden, we were on a street that wasn't on the map with no idea how we got there. But neither of us was really feeling very helpful, so we just sort of kept walking. It was near midnight by the time we found the hostel.

It was on a narrow street of apartment buildings, cheap shoe stores, and seafood restaurants, a tall narrow building with a dirty red and white sign that said HOSTEL LA CUCARACHA.

"Oh, God," I said.

"Come on, rich boy," Suki said.

The lobby was small and dark and stank of old cigarette smoke. Several vinyl couches that were pretty beat up lined the walls, and above them hung a series of pastel still-life paintings. They appeared to have been done by some failed art student disguising his lack of talent by painting in a faux-cubist style. They were possibly the ugliest things I've ever seen. There were travelers sprawled all over the couches, most of them with dreadlocks, all of them speaking English in loud Australian accents. One of them was noodling on a guitar, and pretty much all of them seemed to be smoking and talking at the same time. It was the exact opposite of tranquil.

Behind the counter, there was a doorway with a sign that said INTERNET over it. For a minute, I considered rushing in there for any news of Flan. Or—shudder—Rob. But then I realized that bad news could be extremely crushing right now, so I killed the urge and silently followed Suki up to the front desk.

An older woman with gray bags under her eyes sat behind the counter. A cigarette was dangling from her mouth, and she exhaled and inhaled without removing it.

"Oh, God," I said again.

Suki rolled her eyes and said, *"Buenas noches."*

A very long moment passed, then the woman behind the counter slowly rolled her eyes up to look. *"Diga . . . ,"* she said, without moving any of her features and drawing the word out long.

"Por favor," Suki said, clasping her hands. *"Por favor, una habitación para dos personas."*

"Habitación privada?" the woman asked. I was pretty sure I understood that one, and stepped forward and nodded yes, looking probably more crazed than I'd meant to. The woman stared at me for a moment, and then turned back to Suki.

"Bueno. Treinta euros, señorita."

Suki nodded and put the money on the counter. The woman handed her a key and her change and said, *"Numero dieciocho. El piso tercero. Buenas noches."*

I turned the edges of my mouth upward in Suki's direction, doing my best to convey relief. She sighed disgustedly, and we headed up to see what La Cucaracha had in store for us.

There's always a party at Patch's

"Everything's going to turn out fine." Patch said this more for Greta's benefit than out of any personal conviction. He did have to smile a little at the irony of the crew losing Jonathan, when Jonathan was usually the one going on about how they'd lost him, Patch, and how stressful that was. But Patch also just sort of knew that Jonathan cared more about comfort, and, well, *things*, and that it was going to be really tough for him being out there in the world.

They were walking through the halls of the ship at night, heading for Patch's cabin. The floor shifted with the water underneath their feet. They'd turned the ship upside down looking for Suki—computer lab, late-night snack bar, every corner of the deck. They'd combed the halls of every level and knocked on every door they could think of. Nobody had seen them.

Greta nodded at Patch's reassurance, but she still looked pretty worried. Patch realized that the only times he'd seen Greta, she'd been with Suki, or looking for her.

"Listen, at least they're not alone. I'm sure they ran into each other on the dock. We're not going to land in Barcelona till the day after tomorrow. They can probably get a ferry, or maybe even a flight by then. J probably has his dad's credit card and cash, which should cover it no problem. They'll figure it out."

"But maybe Barker could do something . . . ?"

"If we tell Barker, he'll kick them off the trip. This way, maybe they can still get back on. Nobody'll know the difference."

"I guess."

They were coming to one of the remote, upper level cabins and they could hear music. It smelled a little like smoke, too, which was weird.

"Isn't that Prince?"

"Um . . . ," Patch said as he reached for the knob of his door. By this time, it was pretty obvious that his cabin was the source of the music.

Greta lowered her eyes sheepishly. "I think Suki might have mentioned something about you having a party tonight. She might have, uh, mentioned it to a couple of other people, too . . ."

Patch pushed through the door and into what would surely go down as *the* party of Ocean Term 2005. His bathtub had been filled with ice and this strange Spanish beer that someone had bought a truckload of in Mallorca. Some kid had whipped out his iBook and was now perched on Patch's desk playing the role of self-appointed deejay. Everyone was dancing, except those couples that had slipped off to the corners to discreetly hook up. And Mickey Pardo, God bless him, was on the bed singing along to "Little Red Corvette," and pretending to drive. This mime was (not surprisingly) both convincing, and somewhat perverse.

"Mickey!" Patch hollered over the crowd. The music was really loud, and Patch wasn't sure Mickey would even hear him.

Mickey turned to them, pretending to shift into a faster gear and sort of slap the imaginary steering wheel. "Move over, baby, gimme the keys," he mouthed at them, "I'm gonna try to tame your little red love machine. Little Red Corvette! Baby, you're much too fast . . ."

Mickey jumped off the bed and came over to them. He looked Greta in the eyes and shrieked, "Yes, you are . . ." along with the song. Then he cackled and threw his head back. When he brought his eyes back on them, it was as though Prince had disappeared and he'd been transformed into Mickey again. "What's *up*, dudes?"

"Who are all these people?"

"I dunno. Didn't you invite them? I had to hear about your party from Greta. Which, no offense—"

"None taken."

"—was lame."

"Dude, *I* didn't invite them. I just invited Arno and I was going to invite you and Jonathan, and—"

"Oh, speaking of J," Mickey said, "did you ever find Suki?"

Greta shook her head.

"They definitely got left on Mallorca," Patch said.

"Holy shit."

Just then, Arno came through the door.

"Where the hell have *you* been?" Mickey asked, shaking his head in disgust because he already knew the answer. It had been about an hour since Arno left.

"Sara-Beth got, um . . . sick . . ."

"Sara-Beth Benny?" Patch asked.

"Yeah, I had to take her back to her cabin."

They all took this in for a minute.

Then Patch said: "Anyway, though, I was just saying that we've looked everywhere they could possibly be on this ship, and we're pretty sure that both Suki and J got left on Mallorca."

"That's impossible," Arno said, laughing to himself. "There's no Prada on Mallorca."

"There is, actually," Greta offered. "I read about it in *W*."

"Oh."

"I think it's going to be okay, though. But we should get all these people out of here, and come up with a plan."

Greta cleared her throat and stepped forward. The guys watched in surprise as she cupped her hands around her mouth, and screamed: "All right, everybody. This is a raid. Anyone still in this room in ten minutes will be subjected to drug and alcohol testing . . ."

The kid with the iBook slammed his computer shut and dashed for the door. The room fell silent; then everybody started to run. The stampede forced Patch and Greta to one side of the door, and Mickey and Arno to the other. As they watched the last of the party-goers go off in search of another cabin, Mickey leaned over and whispered to Arno:

"Suki's friend is kind of really hot."

My nightmare has just begun

"This isn't *so* bad," Suki said, after we finally jammed open the door to our room. I wasn't sure if she was trying to patronize me or make me feel better. Number eighteen was on the top floor, in a dank corner that smelled of cigarette smoke. The room looked like some monk or other had just spent his final years slowly dying here. The walls were dark wood, the floor was linoleum, and the windows were shuttered. Over the smallest double bed I've ever seen hung a simple and gigantic cross. I'm not particularly religious or anything, but crosses like that still weird me out a little. I sat down on the bed, and then I realized that everything was going to get much worse.

"This bed is so uncomfortable."

"Hey, at least we got a room," Suki said, undoing the window latch and pushing open the shutters.

"Have you touched the bedspread?! Touch it.

It's like sandpaper."

"It can't be that bad." Suki leaned out the window and looked at the scene below. "This is actually pretty. Come look. There's a little square down below."

The last thing I wanted to see was a pretty little square. It was just going to remind me that we had been abandoned in a foreign country with no finances and no clean clothes.

"Maybe later," I said, and went into the bathroom and flipped on the light. As the neon lights stuttered on, I was met with a very harried, cranky-looking vision of myself. I tried to give my reflection a little talking-to: *This is an adventure, it's romantic.* If only I had a few credit cards, a plane ticket out of here, and Flan, it could actually be sort of awesome. The thought of Flan gave me a little kick, like a sort of renewed zeal to get the hell out of here. I had to get back and protect her from Rob. I used the dry bar of cheap soap to clean up my face, and a dab of the cheap conditioner to get my hair back into form, took a deep breath, and went back into the monk's cell.

Suki was sitting on the windowsill, staring up at the night sky and smoking one of those weird cigarettes. It smelled like a harem in there, and it was actually a kind of romantic picture.

"I quit this morning," she said without looking at me, "but this seems like a pretty good reason to start again."

"Hey," I said, trying to sound conciliatory. Suki didn't respond, so I went on. "So, in the morning, I'll call my mom and get her to wire us some money."

"In the *morning*? In the morning, it'll be the middle of the night in New York."

"Um, no. It's six hours ahead there, so if we wake up at eight it will be like two there."

"No, they're six hours *behind.* If we wake up at eight—which is doubtful—it will be two in the morning there."

"Oh." Could that be right? Then Rob *hadn't* been at Flan's at two in the morning! This was good, this was very good. I cleared my throat. "Should we try and call now?"

"I don't think we can get a phone card anywhere at this time of night. And besides, I'm exhausted. Let's just wake up fresh in the morning, figure out what we need to do, and then try and get some money."

This sounded sensible, so I nodded and sat down next to her on the windowsill.

"Listen," Suki said, "I'm really sorry, but my parents are on this retreat in Provo where they take a vow of silence and don't speak for three weeks. So I don't think I'm going to be able to get any money from them to get us out of here." She bit her lip when she said this, which struck me as needlessly coy, especially since I already told her that I'd pay for us to get to Barcelona.

It reminded me why I so disliked this girl in the first place: She'd been a total tease with my guys. I know this lame, narcissistic type of girl pretty well. New York is full of them, except the better-dressed version. She'd created all this tension between Arno and Mickey, just because she wanted everybody drooling over her all the time.

All I said was: "That's cool. My mom's pretty easy to track down, and it shouldn't be a problem to wire us plenty of cash."

"Thanks."

I nodded to let her know it was no problem, and Suki blew smoke rings out the window. "I think what we do is, tomorrow, we check out of our hotel and find a ferry schedule and see what time the ferries run to Barcelona. When it's morning in New York, we call and get some money transferred, and then we get on the next ferry outta here. Ocean Term is going to be doing their survival test all tomorrow, anyway, and hopefully we can sneak back onto the ship without anyone being the wiser. If, that is, they haven't found us out yet," she said.

"My guys will be covering for us."

"Yeah, Greta, too."

"Sounds like a good plan."

Suki took several slow drags of her cigarette and I thought about how maybe my assessment of her was too harsh. Which was a charitable thought I had way too soon.

"Well, I'm glad you had a chance to redo your hair," she said.

"What's wrong with my hair?" I said defensively.

Suki shrugged.

"*You're* the one running around with this Pocahontas look. I mean, you're really one to talk about colonization when you're pretending to be an Indian. Oops, sorry, *Native American*."

"Pocahontas?! Just because I'm a woman of color doesn't make me a 'Pocahontas'"—she was making the air quotes again—"I mean, that's just *so typical*. Like any ethnic woman with braids— which by the way is a hairstyle that women of hundreds of cultures have worn over thousands of years—*must* be an Indian. Of *course*."

We stared at each other furiously. Suki jammed out her cigarette and lit another one.

"It's going to reek in here," I said, not even trying for nice.

"You know, Jonathan," she said, taking a drag, "you're the perfect example of this theory I have about the difference between men and women."

Oh, God. I could guess where this was going, and it was not going to be anything I hadn't heard before. Then she smiled (wickedly, I think) and pulled a bottle of wine out of her beach bag.

"Vino?"

And I felt like, Yeah, I do need some *vino*. I shrugged.

"I bought this as a gift for my parents. But I think I could probably use it more then them right now." Suki took a small buck knife out of the bag. Placing the cigarette between her lips, she quickly skinned the wrapper off the bottle's neck, jammed the blade into the cork, put the bottle between her knees, and wrenched the knife out of the bottle. Incredibly, there was no spill or breakage. She held the knife up, with the cork on the end of the blade, for me to see. Taking the cigarette out of her mouth, she said, "Yes!" in triumph.

"That was quite a show."

"Yes, which brings me to my theory," she said, taking a swig and then passing me the bottle.

"What's that?" I took a swig. It was not entirely bad wine.

"I think men are the peacocks, and females are the truly tough sex."

"Just because I care about my hair . . ."

"It's not about your hair. And don't be such a narcissist. It's not about just you. Dudes are at heart sensitive, and women are at heart strong and resilient. It's just that guys always talk louder, because of history and, you know, all of that, and women are just so good at suffering in silence."

"Oh, come on. I'm a modern guy, okay? I'm not a sexist or whatever else you're gonna call me. But guys still have to do all the hard stuff. They have to ask girls out, and they have to be confident, and they have to know, like, which restaurants to go to. Girls can just smile and get away with shit . . ."

"*Women* do not 'get away with shit.' They *let* dudes get away with shit. Who gets their period every month? Who gives birth?"

Suki stared at me with an incredulous, gaping expression that revealed a mouth of perfectly straight, gray red-wine teeth. Gross. The wine bottle was about half empty by now, and we were definitely on our way to finishing it. The conversation continued to get more heated, and spin more out of control. Then Suki stormed out of the room.

The fastest way to make Jonathan freak out is . . .

From: santananumerouno@yahoo.com
To: jonathanm@gissing.edu

My Dear Jon:

I know we hate each other on Mama's yacht, but I want to write you and tell you it is done. I am sleeping in your brother Ted's room, and is very nice and your mother is treating me like sun. David is my friend now, he show me total the city. I show him other things about the city to him he no no yet. Also we meet Patch's sisters February and Flan. (Flan is sweet as flan! Ha ha!) Now we are good friends too. We all in the bed last night and so much fun. Understand?

Hasta la vista,

Rob

My head hurts really, really bad

There were bells ringing—church bells? And it sounded like a lot of them. Ten? Eleven? Could it be that late?—and the morning light was slicing through the windows. Thinking about the light caused an instant and awful pain to shoot through the left side of my head, which made me realize that, during the night, my head had been forced into some medieval torture device. That's what it felt like anyway. I sat up, and then had to hold still to keep myself from puking. I was forced to assess my situation. It was not good.

The original wine bottle was sitting on the windowsill, along with numerous cigarette butts. There were beer bottles and many mini liquor bottles strewn across the floor and the chest of drawers. It all started coming back to me—either Suki or I, and I had as yet no memory of which, had stormed out at some point and returned with a couple backpackers from the lobby to back up their point. (Somehow, I suspect this wasn't me.) This turned into many more backpackers, and before long, a whole room of smelly people were debating the gender issue and getting wasted. Not pretty. Luckily, though, only Suki and I were in the room this morning. Suki was beside me, breathing normally and sound asleep.

I went to the bathroom and guzzled tap water (not tasty). What could be done about my hair I did, and what could be done about my clothes, was, well, not a lot. I put them on and slipped out of the room.

I wanted to see if there was any word from Flan by myself, without Suki hovering over me, and I figured I could go down and check my e-mail before she woke up.

I tiptoed down to the first floor, where the same woman was sitting at the desk with her back to me. She didn't turn to look at me, so I just walked into the Internet room. While small and nicotine-saturated, there did appear to be several computers hooked up to the Internet. An attendant-type guy waved me in. So I figured it must be free, and took one of the computers.

I surfed casually for a minute—a couple New York blogs I like to keep up with, whatever. When

I was feeling a little warmed up and more myself, I decided to check my e-mail and see if Flan had written me. But what I found was way worse than no e-mail from Flan. In fact, it was worse than I could have imagined, in a really confusing, hard-to-explain kind of way.

Remember that e-mail from the address I didn't recognize? You guessed it: Rob. He'd written me this e-mail that basically said he was going to get all *Single White Female*, or, what-ever, Single White Male on me, and that he liked Flan, or he thought she was sweet or something, and then he signed off with this dumb threat from an Arnold Schwarzenegger movie. Also, something had happened in a bed, and that threw me into a panic. I seriously considered try-ing to swim to New York, and I was filled with so much adrenaline and fear that I think I maybe could have, too.

This had to be some absurd form of torture. I was stuck on the other side of the world, with no immediate out, and fucking Rob was writing me illiterate e-mails about being friends with my friend and being into my girl. I pictured sweet, big-eyed Flan with skeevy Rob, and regretted the image instantly. I gripped the keyboard and tried to think of what to do. A furious e-mail from a remote location seemed impotent, so I decided the best thing I could do was e-mail David. He could tell me what was going on. And maybe he could sort of watch Flan for me.

I fired off a pleading e-mail to him, my hands hammering out the words without any conscious control. Just as I clicked the SEND button, I heard someone calling my name.

I turned and saw Suki standing in the doorway, her braids carefully redone. She looked irritatingly radiant. "What's the matter? You're pale as a ghost . . ."

She pulled up a chair next to me. Why was she being all nice? This was weird.

"Oh, it's just that . . . I didn't tell you this, but, before I started Ocean Term I was on this yacht, with my dad and new stepmom. Me and all my friends went on a trip on my new stepmom's yacht for their honeymoon. And my new stepbrother, Rob, who is like this total Eurotrash sleazer, came with us too. And now he's in New York, and I just got this e-mail from him and he's living in my apartment and it's just weird is all."

"Oh," Suki said, looking confused. "That *is*

weird. But is that all? You look, you know, spooked."

"Well, you know my friend Patch? His little sister, Flan—she's like, so, um, sweet? Like family, you know, and Rob mentioned her in the e-mail. I think he likes her. I asked my friend David to keep an eye on her for me, so . . . I just, um . . . I mean, I would feel responsible is all if anything happened to her."

"How old is she?"

"Fourteen."

Suki shook her braids off her shoulders and laughed. "Oh, *Jonathan*, I think she can probably take care of herself. Let's go. We've got lots of things to figure out."

Which was pretty much what I should have expected her to say. She grabbed my hand and dragged me out into the city.

"Fuck me. What time is it?"

Patch looked up from the foot of his bed, where he had been sleeping, to see who had spoken. It was Arno, who was leaning against the wall behind the bed. He looked both bored and beat, like he had been half awake for a while. Mickey, lying next to him, snored. On the other side of Patch, Greta was twisted up in a comforter. Her wild, reddish curls were all they could see of her.

"Hey, dude, you know what time it is?" he repeated, seeing Patch stir.

Patch stood up and went into the bathroom for a piss. When he came back out, he picked up the alarm clock and said, "It's eight o'clock, dude. You've been up this early possibly never."

"Easy for you to say. You're exempt from survival hell. We have to leave at, like, ten o'clock."

They smiled at each other faintly, both savoring Patch's absurd luck. "True. That sucks man," Patch said. Then the slow pieces of the here-and-now started coming together in his head. Instead of deciding what to do about Jonathan the night before, they'd all stayed up playing drinking games. Patch's head hurt pretty bad, and he didn't even have to take a survival test. "When do you guys have to be there?"

Greta pushed back the covers and turned toward him. The guys—Mickey, who had been snoring until that very moment, included—all sat up and looked at her then, but she appeared to still be wearing her tank top and conservative boy-short underwear. They all looked away quickly to disguise the blatant stare. Greta cleared her throat and said, "We have to report on deck by nine thirty."

Patch nodded. Then he said remorsefully, "We never figured out what we should do about Jonathan."

"Or Suki," Mickey and Arno said at the same time.

"Or Suki."

"I really hope they'll be able to figure out that they should get to Barcelona," Greta said.

"Not so sure J will, actually," Arno said.

"Well, the only way to get in touch with them is e-mail, really, and the Internet was still down last night. We could go check, I guess . . ."

After a discussion of who should prepare for the survival test (since Greta, Mickey and Arno constituted the remaining members of their group), Mickey and Arno gallantly volunteered to do the boring work of packing their "Survival Kit," and Patch and Greta went to try to send a message to Jonathan.

The lower levels of the ship were abuzz with the other Ocean Term students getting ready for the survival test. As they passed by, the guys nodded at Patch with a sort of distanced respect, and the girls shot weird, competitive glances at Greta. She seemed not to notice them. When they got to the computer lab, they saw a big OUT OF ORDER sign on the door.

"Shoot," Greta muttered as they tried to think what else they could do.

"Maybe Suki called her parents. Do you think we should try and, I don't know, call them?"

"Um . . . they're sort of unavailable right now. Why? Are Jonathan's parents really strict?"

That made Patch smile a little, because strict wasn't really how he'd describe any of their parents. "Nah. She'd be cool—J's mom, I mean—I just can't remember her phone number."

"You don't know your own best friend's *phone number*?"

"Yeah, I don't really spend that much time remembering stuff like that. I mean, I know his *cell* number by heart, and the rest of my guys'. But I guess I haven't called him at home in a really long time . . ."

"Oh."

"I guess we could try to find his mom, though."

"How are we going to figure out her number?"

Patch shrugged. "He might have that written down in his room somewhere?"

"Okay, let's go look."

When they got to Jonathan's cabin, they saw that it was spare and pristine as ever. Definitely nobody had slept there the night before. Patch walked in first, and Greta closed the door behind them.

"Check for his Palm Pilot. I'm sure he brought it with him."

They began looking around for it. There were a pile of papers on the bed, and Patch started going through them. After a few minutes Patch decided they should give up, and he almost got it out of his mouth, too, when he was interrupted by a loud knock and a voice at the door.

"Jonathan?!"

Greta and Patch froze, and stared at each other. A very long moment passed and then Patch called out, in an affected voice, "Ye-es?" It sounded more girly then he'd meant for it to.

The voice continued: "Jonathan, it's Stephanie. Are you okay? The test is today, you know, and your group members say they haven't been in contact with you about it since yesterday morning. They're worried that they need to find a last-minute replacement for you, since the other member of their group is Patch and we all know our hero will be judging instead of competing. Are you still planning on taking the test?"

Patch moved closer to the door, and continued in the ridiculous falsetto that sounded nothing like Jonathan.

"I feel really, really bad. Like, um, seasick. I do want to do a survival, but I'm just not . . . emotionally prepared for it. And I don't think I have the right . . . clothes. Is it too late to sign up for the written exam?"

They heard a twittering laugh through the door. Patch watched as Greta's eyes involuntarily rolled to the back of her head.

"Well, Jonathan, I have to admit I was sort of expecting it. I'll sign you up for the written. You just get your rest."

"Thanks, Steph . . ."

"What?"

"Uh, thanks, Ms. Rayder."

"No problem, Jonathan."

Greta and Patch crept to the door and listened to her footsteps descend down the hall. When they were sure she was gone Patch laughed.

"I didn't know I had any of him in me."

"You really don't," Greta said.

The old keep-an-eye-on-her-for-me

From: grobman@hotmail.com
To: jonathanm@gissing.edu

Hey dude. Got your e-mail. Bummer about missing the boat. That sucks, man. Yeah I know Rob's not so good at English. But he's pretty cool. Since we've been hanging out it's been a really good time. For once I feel like I'm good with girls. Its weird it's like I meet them, and I can talk to them and they seem to want to talk to me. And you're not going to believe this, but we went to this wild Eastern European dance place in Chinatown and it was this wild crowd and everybody was dancing and, this is the weird part, I danced too. It felt good. February was there and after that we went to the Floods and hung out some more. That's how Rob met Flan, it wasn't like he just called her up, so stop writing in all caps, okay? I saw your mom again. She's had a lot of sessions with my dad and she seems really good. Actually, she seems really manic but maybe that's good. She said she's decorating the Fradys and that they gave her all this freedom to do whatever, which is cool. Basketball's sort of ruining my life, but at least it keeps me out of trouble. Ha ha. Anyway though, I understand how you feel about Rob. And don't worry man: I'll keep an eye on Flan for you. See you, David.

P.S. Don't worry about that bed thing. After we went out, we all went to the Floods and watched movies in Flan's bed but it wasn't anything you know dirty. Don't trip.

Trouble follows me around

Of course my mom would be impossible to reach at a time like this.

I had been walking around all afternoon with Suki, and getting increasingly irritated by her self-consciously sassy attitude toward everything. I tried to talk as little as possible, which seemed to fit her fine since she evidently loved talking. She was still wearing the funny short shorts and the floppy hat, which I'm not even going to go into.

Ordinarily, this would be a really lovely kind of day, but I was so stressed out about how I was going to get myself out of this situation, and also about Flan, and what Rob was doing in Flan's bed, that I couldn't even really enjoy it.

We finally found the ferry for Barcelona, and when Suki came back from talking to the ticket agent she said that we had just missed one ferry, and that there was another one at eight. The tickets were sixty euros each, so Suki's cash wasn't going to get us on the boat. We decided to go buy a phone card and call my mom and try to get her to wire us money quickly, so we could get on the boat to Barcelona that night.

But my mom wasn't picking up at home, or on her cell, or on her work cell. And when I tried my dad's house in London, the butler just said that he and Lady Suttwilley were in the Cotswolds, staying in a bed-and-breakfast that didn't have a phone, and wouldn't be reachable for another ten days. So it was my mom or nothing. It had to have been like three o'clock when I started trying to call her, and it was seriously like six or something when we finally trudged back to the hostel sort of stunned and without any clue what we could do next. My throat was sore from pleading so much on her various voicemails.

And that was when I got this weird e-mail from David, which was comforting in theory but was, in actuality, so *not* comforting. It seemed like maybe he was mad about getting kicked off the trip or something, which made me feel bad, but there was nothing I could do from where I was right then so I just e-mailed him like ten times asking where the fuck my mom was.

Suki and I sat in the hostel's Internet room for hours. Suki stared at the cracks in the wall and braided and unbraided her hair, and I quit and reopened my e-mail account about twenty thousand times, hoping for some better news. It goes without saying that I hadn't gotten anything from Flan.

And that's when some big mean dudes tried to pick a fight with me.

"Aye!"

I turned around and saw a huge dude wearing a fishing hat and a gigantic pack on his back. "Aye! Do you think you own this place, mate?" His voice was loud, and he had an Australian accent. We peeked around him. It seemed that there were a whole bunch of other Australians waiting behind him. "How about giving somebody else a go?"

"Look, we're in sort of a situation, and it's imperative that I keep checking my e-mail, okay? So just wait for one of the other computers, and we can all be friends."

"Impair your ass! Who do you think you are?" the Australian muttered. Another one of them took a look at us and said, "New Yorkers—they think they own the whole world."

"Actually, I'm not from—" Suki was cut off by the Australian front man stepping aggressively toward us. The guy was really in my personal space now. As I contemplated a way to explain this to him without sounding snippy, the guy reached between Suki and me and quit my e-mail program.

"That was unnecessary!" Suki said.

"Not as unnecessary as pretty boy playing on the Internet for two hours."

"Cool it. The kid's finished when he's finished."

The Australian froze, then looked over our shoulders to see where the voice had come from. "Says who?"

We all looked. Smiling maniacally, and sitting in an elaborate, cross-legged swami pose at the computer next to us, was the Savage. The tribal tattoo body paint was mostly wiped off now, but there was still some on his face, and he was still wearing the loincloth and crown of twigs. He was even taller and skinnier than I had realized the other day when I'd found Suki yelling at him. "Says I!" he exclaimed dramatically, and bugged out his eyes.

The Australians were evidently impressed.

They stepped back and made gestures with their hands that seemed to indicate that I could take as long as I wanted.

"Um, thanks," I said.

"Yeah, sure," the guy said with a bored American voice. "Those guys are dicks."

"Oh, my God, it's the Orientalist," Suki said.

"Uh, are you on your way to work?" I asked, hoping that if I spoke soon enough the Savage would ignore Suki and maybe not realize that she had been the one screaming at him in the street the yesterday. The Savage looked down at himself and cackled. "No, coming from, actually."

"Do you live here?"

"Nah, I've been traveling all over for a lot of years. I'm from West Orange, New Jersey, originally, but I'm sort of a wanderer, if you know what I mean." The Savage caught Suki staring, so he added: "This is just something I do for spare coin, little lady, so don't you worry your pretty little head about it."

"I'm Jonathan," I said, again trying to distract him from Suki, who I'm sure was warming up for some words about that "little lady" comment.

"Rhett," the Savage said. I looked at him closer and realized that, under the body paint, he had the blue eyes of a WASPy American boy. He reached out his hand to shake mine, and he looked at my wrist. "Nice watch."

And you won't believe it, but I fell for this one. My dad gave me the watch as a sixteenth birthday present, and it's one of my top ten favorite things. It's Tiffany, manly, but still subtle. It says I have places to be, and even if I'm not going to arrive on time, I need to know how long I've kept the son of a bitch waiting. Also, my initials are carved in the back. I immediately warmed to the Savage. Suki was going on, behind me, about her opinion of guys who called her "little" twice in one sentence, so I calmly asked her to wait for me outside and then I showed the Savage a picture of Adrien Brody wearing the same watch at Lotus on a blog that tracks celebrity fashion.

"That," the Savage said, "is a classy watch."

I shrugged and thanked him.

"I bet you could get two thousand euros for that watch."

I gave him a look that said, *Under no circumstances will I sell my watch.*

He smiled genially and spread his hands out reassuringly. "No pressure—Jonathan, is it? I only ask because"—here he cleared his throat and lowered his voice—"I overheard you and your girlfriend talking, and I understand you're in a bit of a tough spot. I think I might be able to help."

I thought about correcting him on the girlfriend part, but then decided it was wiser to just listen. The Savage continued:

"I know of a dogfight that is going to happen in thirty minutes. If I put your watch on El Luchador, we could double its worth."

Everything I know about dogfights comes from that movie *Amores Perros*, which is to say, I don't know a whole lot. But it's seemed pretty brutal in the movie, so I said, meekly, "I think I may be ethically opposed to that kind of cruelty to animals."

The Savage nodded and scratched his chin. "I understand. I also know of a turtle race, at about the same time."

"A *turtle* race?"

"You know, sea turtles. On the beach. It's an old tradition in Mallorca, lots of money changes hands. There's a turtle, El Viejo, even better odds than Luchador. What do you say?"

"This El Viejo . . . he's a sure thing?"

"Absolutely."

"You think we could get four thousand for it?"

"Yes. I'd want to keep a half of the profits, of course."

I nodded, and fingered my wrist.

"We'll have your watch back in one hour, tops."

"How can I know you're not ripping me off?" I asked plaintively.

"Here, you hold this until I come back. Without it, I can't leave the country." The Savage handed me his passport. I looked at the picture inside, of a blond, blue-eyed guy, and then back at the Savage. Despite the face paint, I recognized the long, whittled features. His full name was Rhett Anthony Turner, and he was twenty-four.

I looked at the crumbling walls and the full ashtrays, and considered the possibility that I might seriously have an asthma attack if we stayed here another night. I thought of that awful room, and I slipped the watch off my wrist and handed it to the Savage.

The Savage smiled at me as he took it.

"You and I will dine richly this evening, my friend," he said, and then he was gone.

Arno prefers to be in the lead

At eleven o'clock, Barker gave a good-luck speech and the Ocean Term survival test officially began. He blew a whistle, and all the boats started across the water. Arno worked his oars in unison with Mickey, moving their dinghy out into the open ocean. Greta was sitting on the prow of the little boat, studying the map of Barker Island that Stephanie had given them. The sky was grayer than it had been for days, and the island where they were heading rose, rocky and unwelcoming, before them. Still, in contrast to all that stormy blue, Greta's wind-tossed, hennaed hair looked warm and gorgeous. As though she sensed Arno watching her, she looked up from the map and smiled shyly. Then she looked over his shoulder at the *Ariadne*, where they could still see Patch and Barker watching from deck.

When they'd signed in that morning, Greta had explained to Stephanie that Suki wasn't feeling well enough to take the test, adding that Suki and Jonathan had shared a paella on Mallorca that may not have been so fresh, and that it was possible that they both had food poisoning. Stephanie seemed to buy this. She gave the group's map to Greta and repeated the areas in which they could earn points: the race to the island, setting up camp, teamwork, and the swimming race back. They could confer with other teams, but could only score points for their own team, individually.

Their little boat, which Mickey had nicknamed the *Greta*, advanced through the water. All around them, the other survival teams rowed their boats toward the island. Arno thought to himself how well Mickey and he worked together when they wanted to; they were strong and they were taking the lead. Arno flexed his muscles and pushed.

Greta arched an eyebrow and spread the map across her knees. "So I think the best landing place is going to be on the southeast corner of the island. It looks like there's a beach there . . ."

Mickey was sitting with his back to Greta, and he had barely heard her. He was staring furiously at Arno, who only the day before had been dogging him whenever possible to come out ahead with Greta's best friend. Mickey got mad all over again about Arno telling Suki about Philippa, and then he realized what he probably should have realized yesterday: They were all together for just two weeks on a cruise ship, anyway, and none of them were doing anything but casually hooking up. What the hell did it matter if he *was* on a rebound? And now Arno was apparently interested in Greta, who—Mickey realized suddenly—he was completely into, too. Arno gave him a very innocent look and said, to both of his teammates, "The southeast corner is perfect."

Mickey began to row intensely, almost like he was trying to throw Arno off. Arno matched him, though, and for a while this worked. They rowed furiously, in silence, through the mile of water that lay between the *Ariadne* and Barker Island. They soon took the lead and maintained it for a good long stretch. They were still in the lead as they approached the island. Greta called out to them that they would have to veer east if they were going to land on the beach, but by that time Arno and Mickey were engaged in a war of wills that prevented them from paying much attention to anyone else. Mickey abruptly stopped rowing, and one of the oars shot up while the other plunged into the water.

At first, Arno overcompensated, rowing even harder to try and keep the suddenly much heavier boat moving forward. Then he got pissed, and stood up.

"What are you *doing*?"

"What are *you* doing?"

"Guys . . . ," Greta said softly from behind them. At

the sound of her voice they both sat down. Mickey fished his oar out of the water, and they began rowing again. But Arno was irritated by Mickey's childishness, and he wasn't really paying attention to anything but lifting and pushing the oars. When he heard Greta's voice again, he looked up and realized that they were really close to the island, but they had veered away from the beach and had entered a rocky cove. Greta stood up for a better view, and Mickey gave one last big row. The dinghy glided forward and smacked into a rock, a few feet below the water's surface. Arno looked up to see Greta lose her balance and go flying into the water ahead of them. Then the boat capsized, and he and Mickey were under water, as well.

They treaded water for a few seconds, dealing, again, with the surprising roughness of the ocean. Mickey grabbed the boat and righted it, and held it steady as Arno dived, got a hold of their pack of survival stuff, and resurfaced. They swam toward shore, Arno with the pack and Mickey dragging the boat. Mickey, a few lengths behind, stopped suddenly and called out:

"Where's Greta?"

Arno treaded and looked around. For a minute he didn't see her, and then he did, floating facedown in the water a few lengths behind him. He pushed through the water, pulled her head out of the water, and gently slapped her face. She appeared to be unconscious.

Arno wrapped her arm around his shoulder and, using his right arm to hold her head above water and his left arm to propel them forward, moved toward shore.

He straggled up on the beach behind Mickey, who had pulled the dinghy out of the water. He laid Greta's limp body on the sand.

"Is she okay?" Mickey asked.

"I dunno. She seems to be breathing, but she looks like maybe she hit her head or something?"

"We need to get her warm."

"How?" Arno interjected. "The matches are all soaked and useless now."

"Oh, right."

"I guess I should give her CPR just, you know, in case."

"What? She's breathing, you moron. *Now* try and think of another reason to slobber all over her."

Arno pushed Mickey on the shoulder, and Mickey looked like he was about to take a swing, when Greta's eyes fluttered open and she started giggling.

"Just kidding!" She laughed. "I'm fine. Good to know you two are paying attention."

Arno and Mickey stood there, dripping and wondering what to do, when Stephanie came buzzing around the cove. She was with another of the faculty advisors, who was driving the motorboat, and Patch. As they approached, Arno realized that Stephanie was clapping. Patch gave him a "sorry, nothing I can do for you, dude" look from behind her.

Their boat idled for a second off shore, as Stephanie finished clapping. It was only then that Arno realized she wasn't making fun of them. She took out a bull-horn, and called:

"Great teamwork, sailors! I can't give you guys points for winning the race, but I'm going to give you five merit points for Arno's daring rescue. Congratulations! Good luck."

The motorboat made a roaring-motor noise, and they were gone, leaving Mickey and Arno alone with their feelings. And Greta.

I get through to New York, in the worst possible way

I came out of the Internet room feeling strangely buzzed. Yes, I had missed the boat and was stuck on a strange island in a foreign country. Yes, I was without credit cards or money. But I was betting on a turtle fight—a *sea* turtle fight—which would ensure me a comfortable night in one of the island's premier establishments and a safe trip home. How cool was I?

Suki was sitting in the lobby with her arms across her chest and staring at the ceiling.

"I'm glad you've rid yourself of that bigot," she said as I came out.

"Uh-huh. Anyway, I'm going to try the phone one more time. Wait here, okay?"

"Yeah, but it's almost seven o'clock. I don't think we're making that ferry. Should I get us a room for another night?"

"Nah, I have a plan. We're going to stay

someplace nice tonight, and tomorrow we'll get the early boat for Barcelona and we'll get into the city well before Ocean Term does."

"But how . . . ?"

"*Trust* me."

She made a face and sat down.

I went out to the pay phone down the street from the hostel. All the shutters on the little winding street were open, and for once I took a minute to look up at all the wrought-iron work on the old buildings. It smelled like a lot of people's dinners were being prepared. I felt good, and I thought, no way could a guy like Rob take Flan away from a guy like me. I resolved to call her, and set the situation straight.

I dialed the familiar number of the house on Perry Street and listened to the normal, comforting American dial tone. It rang five times, and then a guy's voice picked up and said:

"Talk to me." It was Rob. My heart lurched. He was still *there*?

I fought the impulse to slam the phone down, and told myself that the only way I could figure out what was going on was to play nice. It was also the only way I was going to find out where the hell my mom was.

"Rob, I'm glad I finally got ahold of you."

"Jon-a-tin! I've been missing you. Did you get my e-mail?"

"Uh, yeah, yeah, it was good to hear from you. Sorry I've been so out of touch, this program is, like, really hectic."

"Su-pair! Cute girls?"

"Um, sort of. Listen. Have you seen my mom?"

"Yes, I'm staying with her! I love your apartment. Très chic."

"But recently. Like have you seen her yesterday or today."

"No. Because, she went to a ranch."

"A ranch?!"

"Yes. *Cómo se llama.* Canyon, *pienso que sí*, Canyon Ranch."

"Oh, *dammit*." I should have guessed this. My mom always goes on some weight-loss or detox retreat in January. "When did she leave?"

"Yesterday. Jon-a-tin, what is the matter?"

I drew in a deep breath. I was really, really hating this guy, and it wasn't easy to hide it. "Listen, this bad thing happened and I got separated from the trip. Which would be fine, except that I forgot my wallet on the boat."

171

"*No!* Where are you?"

"Mallorca."

"Oh, I *love* Mallorca. Ibiza is far better, but Mallorca, very good."

"I'm sure it's lovely. But I need to get some money or I'm screwed. Did my mom leave you a number where she can be reached?"

"Hmmmm . . . I think so. At home maybe. But I don't have it with me."

I slapped my forehead.

"But you need money now, anyway, right? I'll go home tonight and get the number at the ranch and e-mail it to you. But in the meantime, I just wire you some money so you can get a hotel room, okay?"

Moronic as this may seem, my impulse was to tell him forget it, I just bet one of my favorite possessions on a sea turtle named El Viejo, I don't need your help. But that of course was not what I did.

"Are you sure? That would be great," I said, although in my head I was screaming, *What are you doing with Flan?!*

"Yeah, easy, how you say, no sweat? The Western Union is on Calle Aragon in the center of town. Every time I lose my wallet on Mallorca,

Mama wires me some money there. They're always open until eight during holiday. I'll call right now, and you should be able to pick it up before they close."

I looked at my wrist, then remembered that my watch wasn't there anymore. But then, as though someone up there might actually be looking out for me, the cathedral rung quarter past seven.

"Thanks, man. I mean, I really appreciate it," I said, although in my head it was, *Flan would never like a sleazy bastard like you!*

"Jon-a-tin, it is nothing. We are brothers."

A voice came on, telling me I was out of minutes. I must have wasted them all trying my mother four thousand times.

"Yeah, well. This is super nice of you." *You backstabbing piece of shit!*

"No sweat. Ha ha!" *You already said that, you imbecile.*

When we hung up, I went back into the lobby. Suki was sitting exactly as before. When I walked in, she said, "Jonathan, let's just get a room here for the night. I'm going to turn cranky real soon."

"No way. We've got so much cash coming to us. We're sleeping in style tonight."

Suki rolled her eyes. "Yeah, right."

"Listen, I've got to get to the Western Union before they close. You stay here, okay? The Savage is going to drop something for me. Give him this"—I handed her the passport—"and take whatever he has for you. And then wait for me."

She let out one of those grunts of disgust that only girls can do effectively.

"Trust me," I said for the second time that evening.

"Fine. I mean, what are my options?"

I nodded in agreement with her. She had no options.

"Whatever you do, don't leave this place," I called as I ran down the street.

It took me a while, but I found the Western Union. There was a line, of course, but I got there just in time. It was five after eight when a lovely, dark-eyed Spanish girl counted fifteen hundred in crisp euros for me and placed them on the counter.

"You are Rob Santana's brother?" she asked, obviously impressed.

I shrugged. "I guess you could say our families merged, yeah."

"He is one of the wildest visitors," she said in her sweet, accented English. "Whenever he comes to town, crazy stories start going around. He's with a different girl every season. You'll tell him to call me next time he visits, won't you?"

Not what I wanted to hear. Why couldn't she see Rob the way I did, as a slimy guy who was really, really short on class? Flan would, right? I smiled weakly and promised to give Rob her number, and ran down the street back to the hostel. I fought the image of Rob as a romantic party boy the whole way. But if the lovely girl in the Mallorca Westen Union fell for the act, how would little Flan Flood hold up?

I almost managed to put it out of my mind. After all, everything was about to work out. I had fifteen hundred euros in my hand, and I was about to get three thousand more. By the time I huffed into the hostel lobby, I had psyched myself up again.

My rally died when I saw Suki.

She looked up at me furiously and didn't say a word.

"Did the Savage come?" I asked.

"*Oh*, yeah."

"Did he bring me an envelope or a package or something?"

"Yup. He had an envelope. He took it out, and

he showed me all this money inside, and he said, 'Here you go, little lady. You give this to Jonathan, and now why don't you and I go for a dance.' Well, I told him, 'I am *not* that kind of lady.'"

"What happened to the envelope?" My voice was very small.

"I threw that passport at him and told him to go shove it. Which is what I'd like to tell *you* to do! I can't believe you think a fancy hotel room justifies pimping me out!"

"Where'd the Savage go . . . ?"

"Gone to hell I hope. You go, too, for all I care!"

I put my face into my hands and tried not to cry. I took several deep breaths, and then looked up expecting to see a very confrontational Suki.

I was wrong. Her mouth was frozen in a small, diminutive O shape and her face had gone white. We looked at each other for a long, frightened moment.

"Wait, pimping a girl out, that wouldn't really occur to you, would it?"

I shook my head, 'cause no, it really wouldn't.

Mickey's a survivor

As soon as Mickey saw the fish, he knew it was his. The water had gone tranquil and turquoise in the afternoon, and from the surface you could see nearly to the bottom. Mickey was on one of the rocky outcroppings that had ejected them from their boat earlier in the day. He stepped to the edge, let out a war whoop, and dove headfirst through the water and toward the fish. Of course, once he was a good ways under water he realized that the fish was not only much larger than it had originally appeared, but that it was a shark. A very small shark—only a foot and a half or so—but it still had frightening teeth inside its little mouth.

Well, Mickey thought, now's as good a time to go as any, and he threw his arms around the shark and began kicking his way back up to the surface. The shark squirmed mightily in his arms, but once Mickey had gotten some air in his lungs, he put an end to the wrestling match by hitting the shark on the nose with his forehead. This was what his third-grade teacher had told him to do if he ever came face-to-face with a shark, and, absurdly, it worked. Mickey grabbed the stunned creature by its tail and swung it so that its head struck the rock with a fatal *thwap!* Then he tossed the lifeless fish into the dinghy and rowed back to shore.

He found the camping spot they had chosen earlier. It was on a high, dry space above the beach, with a good view of their ship. The sun was going down, and all along the rocky face of the island little fires were being lit with dry matches by other Ocean Term students. Greta had collected a bunch of palm fronds and sticks, and had managed to make a sort of tent out of them. She was kneeling on the ground and bending over to make sure the sticks she used for poles were secure. There was dirt on her tank top and cutoff jeans and she looked very wild and capable and like she would be down for pretty much anything. She looked primitive, in fact. Looking at her made Mickey feel all randy.

Meanwhile, Arno had collected rocks in a fireplace formation and had formed a burnable pyramid of twigs and kindling. He was blowing on their matches, which had of course been ruined when they all fell out of the boat earlier. He looked really out of his element, and Mickey imagined how much fun it would be to stomp on his head. Then he could carry Greta up to the highest point on the island and they could offer themselves to the gods, or something else very Aztec.

"Guess what's for dinner," Mickey called. Arno looked up at him with a seriously pissed expression. When Mickey threw the shark down in front of him, Arno stared at it, and then turned his face up to Mickey bitterly.

"How exactly are we going to cook that, genius?"

"Dude, I don't know but I don't think *blowing* on the matches is going to dry them out."

"You got a better idea?"

"Actually, yeah."

"Oh, my God, how did you catch that thing?" Greta came over to them, dusting off her hands. Her hair was a mess, and her face was a little sunburned. But her skin had faded over the night so that she mostly looked like she had a decent tan.

"Well, I . . ."

"The real question, and what I said in the first place, is how are we going to *cook* it."

Mickey snorted, then went over to the fire pit. He took a flattened stick and another round stick and rubbed it up and down with a little bit of dried grass until a tiny flame emerged. He pressed the flaming grass carefully into the pyramid, and slowly but surely the whole thing caught on. Mickey fanned it with his wife-beater, which he'd torn off hours ago to let it dry in the sun.

Mickey smiled at Greta like a kid who'd just busted open the piñata. "A little trick my granddad learned during the Cuban Revolution, when he and Che were hiding from Batista's army in the Sierra Maestra."

"That is such a lie." Arno sneered.

"Maybe, but it's fun, which is more than I can say for you, you stuck-up little bitch. Now shut up and cook this thing."

So they set about hacking up the fish with the knife from their survival kit. While they were waiting for the fish to cook, Greta excused herself to pee. Mickey and Arno watched her disappear into the bushes, and then Arno hissed, "Look, out of respect for you I decided to stop going after Suki. Why are you always chasing the girl I'm after?"

"What? You only stopped going after her once she disappeared! Are you insane?"

"I might ask you that question."

They both stood instinctively and stared at each other. Mickey could feel the fury building inside of him, and even though he'd never been in a fistfight—at least, not with one of the guys in his crew—he felt like he might be about to be in one now.

A bright light shone on them just then, like they were in an episode of *Cops* or something, and then they heard Stephanie calling "Good work, sailors!" into her bullhorn. A few moments later, she appeared in their campground. She was wearing a very warm-looking jacket and leggings, and the guy who had been driving the boat earlier came along behind her holding a ridiculously powerful flashlight.

"This is quite a setup!" Stephanie exclaimed, going over to Greta's palm tent and examining it. Mickey and Arno sat down on the log by the fire. She took little notes on a clipboard she carried. She looked over the fire, and the remains of the shark, and made little exaggerated *mmmm-hmmmm* noises.

Greta came back from the bushes and sat between Mickey and Arno as Stephanie finished her report. She strained her neck to see over the other faculty guy, and if there were anybody else in the group. When Stephanie was done, she looked at them cheerily.

"I can't tell you how many points you got, but I can tell you your score is very impressive. All right, sailors, good luck getting through the night!"

When she was gone, Mickey leaned across Greta and shoved Arno off the log.

I love a classy hotel

There was only one thing that was going to make me feel better about the loss of my watch and my general, utter stupidity. That thing was luxury. I took Suki to the Hotel Miramar and I got us a room. The same officious little twit was behind the counter, and he opened his mouth in protest when he saw me coming through the door. I silenced him with something better than a perfect Spanish accent. I put three hundred euro notes on the counter in front of him.

"*Habitación para dos,*" I said. My accent was awful. It felt great.

The concierge smiled a little smile to himself, and then said something in his very fast Spanish.

"*Cómo?*" I asked him.

"The *habitaciones baratas* are all full, señor."

He was obviously relishing this, but I was ready for him. "What *do* you have available?"

The concierge flipped through his reservation

book. "It seems we have the Miro Suite available. Although, I suppose it will be a little *caro* for you."

"We'll take it," I said.

"Five hundred euros, please."

I laid down the bills like they were nothing to me.

Suki, at my shoulder, was strangely quiet and supportive through all of this, probably because she still felt bad about my watch. Which would, you know, make sense.

When I had filled out the guest card, and the concierge had stopped glaring at me, the bellboy appeared. He took us up the rickety, old-fashioned elevator to the fourth floor, unlocked our suite, and let us into just about the most perfect place in the whole world.

There is nothing I love like a good hotel. Your towels and sheets are changed daily, and of course, they allow you to, for a short while, be completely untethered from your life and your personality and whatever awful stuff has been going on with you. Now, you may think, hotel rooms are where thousands of different unkempt people do gross things to themselves and others, so what's clean about that? And that's exactly the sort of thing I think *constantly* when I'm in a hotel like, say, La Cucaracha. When I'm in a good hotel, that never enters my mind. So you can imagine how freaking psyched I was to be out of the one and into the other.

When the bellboy was gone, Suki did what pretty much all girls do when they go into a fancy hotel room. She kicked off her shoes and started jumping on the bed, which was very large and soft-looking and covered in a tasteful cream brocade coverlet. The room was expansive, and it had a chandelier and soft carpeting and big French doors that led out onto a terrace. I checked in the bathroom. There were a lot of mirrors and gold detail, and the tub was gigantic and heart-shaped. There were a lot of expensive-looking products, too: soaps and lotions and hair stuff. And there were two impossibly soft white robes, wrapped in plastic, hanging from the door.

"First bath!" I called. I took my time making myself feel human again, and used one of the pomades to get my hair back into the shape it had been in yesterday morning. The very thought of putting my sweaty clothes back on bummed me out, especially when I noticed that my white cords and T-shirt had taken on a gray tinge. So I put on one of the robes and decided I might never take it off. When I came back into the room, Suki was lying on her back looking very relaxed and staring at the ceiling. Without looking up at me, she said, "What have you been doing, I'm *starving* . . ."

"I know, when did we last eat?"

"I can't remember. I'm gonna take a bath, and then let's order lots of food."

So Suki took a bath, and I went out and took in the view from our terrace, which was pretty fantastic. We faced west, and all along the bay I could see the glittering lights of nightclubs and restaurants and promenades, and all the lovely people enjoying long, lazy nights. Or wild, adrenaline-filled nights, as the case may be. Out beyond the bay, I could see a little corner of open ocean and I imagined that that's where we were headed tomorrow, in a straight line across the water to Barcelona. The situation definitely called for something expensive and drinkable, so I opened the minibar and uncorked a bottle of champagne. I poured us each a glass, and when Suki came out in her white robe we drank it together in silence and enjoyed the cool ocean breeze and the uncompromised comfort of it all.

Then we did what anybody in our situation would do: We ordered American-style omelets with potatoes and toast and a side of pancakes from room service, and we ate breakfast for dinner on the bed in our bathrobes while watching cheesy Spanish television, and periodically making very dramatic accusations and ultimatums (like, "I know you have been making love to the one-legged priest," and, "If you don't murder your lover I will be forced to have an illegitimate child with your father") at each other in gibberish Spanish. As Suki delivered her over-the-top lines, she pulled at the collar of her bathrobe as though she were about to rip it off, and I couldn't help but notice the smooth, pale skin between her perfect little breasts. I wasn't leering or anything, but she was definitely hot, and I began to get why Mickey and Arno were so excited about her.

At some point, there was no more champagne, so we ordered more from room service, and then we danced on the bed and sang "November Rain" at the top of our lungs (she did the words, and I did the guitar solos) and when our champagne flutes were empty we threw them down on the ground and watched them shatter. We thought this was hilarious.

Eventually we collapsed on the very large, very soft bed, and fell asleep.

I wish I could tell you that the rest of our adventure was more of the same and end it here, but that would be a lie.

Arno versus Nature

"What the fuck was that?" Arno had been sleeping fitfully for a few hours, but when he heard the yowl outside the tent, he was definitely awake. Greta and Mickey sat up, and they all peeped outside. Prowling the campsite were four or five mangy-looking dogs.

"Coyotes," Mickey said.

"No, just wild dogs," Arno said. He scooted out from the palm tent and grabbed one of the sticks they had been using to tend the fire. He thrust it into the remaining embers, so that the end caught into flame. He waved it back and forth at the dogs, who howled at him but didn't come any closer.

Arno grabbed one of the many pieces of leftover fish and threw it far into the night.

"Now *git!*" he shouted, sounding more cowboylike than he had meant to. Or than he thought was capable of. The dogs scattered after the fish. Arno took a seat by the fire, feeling revved. He stayed there, long after Mickey and Greta had gone back to sleep. He thought about them in the tent by themselves, and how Mickey might be making a move. He thought about loneliness, and lots of other weighty topics that usually never occurred to him, or, frankly, ever touched on his everyday life. After a while, when he was very tired and convinced that the dogs weren't coming back, he crawled back into the tent and shut his eyes.

He felt beat and capable and much better about himself. As his mind faded into dream, he felt Greta turn in her sleep and curl up against him. *That's right,* he thought, *in their subconscious minds all girls, even the ones with boyfriends, dream of me.*

"All right, sailors, race begins in half an hour!"

The little group camped high above the rocky cove stirred but didn't fully wake for several minutes. Mickey snored lightly, and Greta was still wrapped up in Arno's arms. When Stephanie made her second bullhorn announcement, they all lurched up and quickly assumed some new position. Stepping out of the makeshift tent, they saw that it was still early dawn, the sky rosy and the air crisp and new.

The *Ariadne* was far closer to the island than when the survival test had begun. They could see Stephanie's motorboat circling the island and waking up all the other teams. The staff had collected all the dinghies during the night, and they had to wake up quickly for the race back to shore. Arno felt like something had happened during the night, like he was more focused and competitive and inside his own body now. He also thought that Greta looked entirely adorable, stretching to wake herself up and combing her hair with her fingers.

He watched Mickey moving foggily around the camp. It didn't really seem like competition to Arno.

They stamped out the embers in the fire, collected their survival kit, and headed down to the shore. When Stephanie shouted through the bullhorn, "On your marks. Get set. Go!" They all waded into the water, gasping at the cold and cursing themselves for having signed up for the test.

Perhaps because it was still so early in the day, they concentrated on their swimming and didn't think about the depth of the water, or how tired they were. They swam harder for several lengths, and when the three of them reached the *Ariadne*, in unison, just as the rules instructed, they popped out and saw that they were the first team to arrive. The crew threw down ladders from the top deck and they climbed back up to comfort and safety. When they reached the deck, they saw Barker and his guests, and Patch, who looked deeply bored, behind them.

"Team fifteen!" Barker boomed. "An excellent morning swim! You come in first place for the final segment of the test. Now go get yourselves cleaned up. We have breakfast on the deck in forty-five minutes, and as soon as we get all the teams on board we set sail for Barcelona."

They slapped hands with Patch, and Greta gave him a kiss on the check, and then team fifteen headed to their individual cabins to clean off the cold memory of Barker Island.

When they reached Greta's cabin, Arno put his hand on her waist and said, "You were great today. And you should know that you look gorgeous all wet and flushed like that."

"Uh, thanks," Greta said. Arno winked and started walking down the hall.

Mickey looked after him furiously. He quickly kissed Greta on the cheek and then followed Arno down the hall.

"What the fuck was that?" he shouted after Arno. He didn't turn around, and when Mickey caught up to him he shoved Arno's shoulder. "I said, what the fuck was that?"

Arno did the eyebrow thing at him, which always made Mickey crazy. He ran at the wall behind him, bounced off it, and launched himself into Arno, who

191

artfully dodged him. Mickey smacked into the opposite wall.

Arno continued to walk toward his room, but Mickey came after him growling. "Hey man! What's wrong with you? Why are you always after the girl I like?" he shouted.

"Maybe I *like* her," Arno said, shrugging. He pointed at the door of cabin 164. "That's me. Thanks for keeping up with me in the race today—I was pleasantly surprised, actually." He stepped inside, then waved at Mickey, who looked like he was about to detonate. "Oh, and Mickey? Try and behave yourself."

I am reminded of some of Suki's less attractive qualities

"See? This is totally what I was talking about," Suki said.

I looked down at the silver tray of croissant, café con leche, melon, and orange juice, and felt a familiar irritation spreading from the back of my neck. We hadn't really been talking about anything, and I was still wearing what I was then thinking of as the best bathrobe in the world.

"What? What were you talking about?"

Suki giggled, ripped off a piece of croissant, and threw herself back into the pillows, where she nibbled at the croissant slowly and thoughtfully. Her black hair fanned out around her head.

"Well, it's like when we went on road trips when I was a kid . . . We'd go up to Napa, and drive all those crazy backroads. That was before they got them all fixed for the East Coast wine tourists. Well, my dad and my little brother were *always* the ones who had to 'stop for a breath' and throw up, and my mom and I were always fine and just impatient to get where we were going . . ."

Would you have known what she was talking about? I sure didn't.

"Or it's like that time in anatomy class when we had to dissect cats . . . My partner was a guy and he couldn't handle the smell at all—they keep them in formaldehyde, you know—and he had to go outside while I . . ."

"Okay, I get it. Women are stronger than dudes. So then who got us into this hotel?"

"*Exactly*. I mean, there are all these cultural stereotypes that women are materialistic, and they need to be coddled, and blah blah blah. But look at you! *You* need pampering and comforting, not me. All men really want is to crawl up someplace safe and warm. And women have been accommodating them since the beginning of time."

She seemed to be satisfied that she'd won the argument. So we read the *International Herald Tribune*, which is just as boring as the *New York Times,* because all the articles are basically from the *New York Times*, except there are fewer of them and they're all the international interest ones about how, like, some beer maker in southern Germany whose family has made beer the same way for thousands of years is finally going out of business because of globalization and how sad that is.

Then we got dressed in our old dirty clothes and Suki suggested we go out the back way, because maybe then we could avoid paying our room service bill, and it was probably smarter to save our money. I agreed, even though this seemed really wrong to me, especially since I had plenty of money, just not on me. And what if I wanted to come back here with a girl sometime, like Flan, and see what Mallorca was like when I wasn't all stressed? But Suki was being her old, bossy self again, so we went down the back way all shifty like she wanted to. Before we did, I snuck two of the nice big hotel towels into her bag, just in case.

That was when we saw the boutique. It was tucked into one of the back corners of the first floor, between the restaurant and the pool. A very short, older Spanish woman was sitting on a stool inside smoking and looking imperious. She was wearing an impeccable Chanel suit, and her hair was pulled back severely into a gigantic bun.

Her eyebrows were drawn on in dramatic coal, and her eyelashes were thick, black, and definitely fake. I nudged Suki, and she reluctantly followed me in.

As I looked over the couple pairs of designer jeans and T-shirts they stocked in the men's section, Suki charmed the saleslady in Spanish. I admitted to myself that there was no way to acquire a new outfit and tore myself away, but by that time the shopkeeper and Suki had decided that Suki looked absolutely *preciosa* in a dusky pink Prada sundress. I don't know how we pulled it off (mostly because it was transacted in Spanish), but somehow we convinced her to charge the Prada sundress, a pair of Allaia jeans, and a D&G T-shirt to our room. After excessive *gracias, gracias,* and *de nada*s, we went and changed clothes in the poolside change room, and slipped through the hedges on the far side of the pool.

Is Patch the new Jonathan?

Banquet tables had been erected on the deck, and a breakfast of eggs, sausage, toast, hot coffee, and juice had been laid out for the Ocean Term students once they cleaned up. Barker took his place once all the students had taken theirs. The minister of tourism and his deputy were at Barker's left, and Stephanie and Patch were to his right. He said a few quick words, congratulating everyone, and then told them to eat. The students loaded their plates and ate as if they had been starving for days. The *Ariadne* moved at maximum speed, and by the time the plates were being cleared she was coming into the port of Barcelona.

Patch had been to Barcelona a couple times. When his dad was in his architecture phase he had brought all the Flood kids there to see the Gaudí buildings, which were all very intricate and covered with mosaic and eccentric detail. But he had never approached it by water, and the city looked much more modern and industrial to him when he came at it this way. The harbor was wide, and huge tankers were crowding up the docks. In the early morning, the whole scene was glittery and futuristic and Patch was caught up in staring.

He snapped out of it when Stephanie stood up next to him and said, "Now to announce the winners."

Patch didn't really care about winners. He felt most comfortable in the limbo of travel, and he had liked the Ocean Term adventure for a while. But some of it was really forced and stupid, and the whole thing was losing his interest. He especially disliked the competitive aspect of it all, which seemed counter to exploring places in a real way. Stephanie announced the first- and second-place winners, and some of the teams in front of him were cheering for themselves.

He looked over to see where his friends were. For a minute he couldn't place them, but then he did and it wasn't pretty. Mickey was jumping up and down and shaking his head like a boxer about to start a fight, and Arno was strutting around him and saying something that didn't look cool. Greta stood up from the table and tried to step in between them, but Arno pushed her away.

"And now, for first prize," Stephanie called out, "will group number fifteen, Greta O'Grady, Arno Wildenburger, and Mickey Pardo, please stand!"

Everyone looked over to where Arno and Mickey were squaring off. Mickey barreled forward, with his head into Arno's chest, knocking him over. There was a gasp from the crowd of students. Then Arno and Mickey were rolling around on the deck, hitting and yelling at each other.

"Stop them!" Barker yelled. Just then the boat stopped with a grunt, and the workers down below began securing it to the dock. Patch ran over and pulled Mickey away from Arno. They all stood panting for a second. Mickey's lips were peeled back, like he might start biting.

"Yo, what are you guys doing?" Patch asked.

Arno straightened his shirt defensively, and Mickey shook Patch off. "Nothing," they both said. Greta came up next to Patch.

"I think at first they were fighting over me," she whispered in his ear. "But then it started being about something else entirely. Mickey started talking about how Arno's mother was a home-wrecker, and then Arno basically said that Mickey's mom was a whore. That's when they started fighting."

"Oh." It occurred to Patch that without Jonathan calling them up all the time and putting out their fires, the crew was really falling apart. He was trying to think of a way to convey this to Mickey and Arno, but then he felt Stephanie's hands on his arm.

"Are you all right?" she gasped.

Barker jogged up behind her, breathing heavily. The minister of tourism was close behind, and Barker seemed to be apologizing under his breath. He looked embarrassed. And furious. Arno stepped forward, smiling. Usually Arno was smooth enough to get himself out of these situations, but in this case he was too out of breath to fend for himself. Mickey howled and ran at him with a closed fist, landing it squarely on Arno's jaw. Arno recovered, and leaped on Mickey, and before long all the kids were cheering them on.

It took a few minutes for Patch and Greta to pull them apart, and by that time Barker was practically frothing at the mouth.

"You ungrateful little brats!" he hissed. "There is no drinking on my ship as you know, but there is also no fighting. I made the mistake of selecting you as the winners of the survival test. You have proved yourselves most unworthy. You are banished! Banished!"

Patch tried to intervene, but Barker waved him away.

"Pardo and Wildenburger, go to your cabins and pack your bags. When this ship sets sail tomorrow, you will not be on it!"

Suki and I simply cannot keep out of trouble

At this point in the trip, I should have figured out that pretty much everything was going to go wrong. But I wasn't prepared for what happened to us at the Mallorca ferry dock.

When we got there, we saw a lot of sunburned people with vacation backpacks sitting on the benches and floors of the ferry building. Suki conferred with the ticket agent, and then asked me for a hundred and twenty euros. I handed it over and she took me aside and explained that, because the royal family was at their vacation residence in Mallorca, there was tightened security and they were only letting one ferry in and out a day. That meant we had to wait for the eight o'clock boat.

"You mean, the Spanish royal family?"

"Yeah." She giggled. "You weren't hoping for Prince William, were you? Just kidding."

I'm not sure what that meant, but I rolled my eyes at her.

"Um, but listen. This is probably fine. They say the trip takes about eight hours, so we'll probably get into Barcelona early tomorrow morning and we should still be able to make it on the boat before it leaves."

"Fine," I said. I had no watch, so I could only guess, from the height of the sun, that it was about ten o'clock, leaving us about ten hours. "What are we going to do until then?"

Suki released one of those pealing little laughs that I could so do without, and she said, "Oh, I don't know, enjoy a gorgeous day in one of the most sought-after vacation spots in the world? Jonathan, *come on.*"

So, for a morning and afternoon, we were proper tourists. We ambled through the twisted streets, reading old signs that described the history of ancient squares and looking up at crooked buildings with precarious-looking wrought-iron balconies. We saw a few little cathedrals, and one really big one, with soaring ceilings and an apse the size of my apartment in New York, and lots of very graphic paintings of horrible things that happened around the time of Christ. For those of you who haven't been, Spain is a very, very Catholic country.

At some point, I told Suki that I had about negative ability to do more sightseeing, so we decided to stroll slowly down the main promenade, where all the shops and things were, and maybe try and get a bite to eat before we got on the ferry. I was focusing on the restaurants we were passing, and trying to decide what looked the least romantic so that nobody would insinuate that Suki and I were a couple again. Suki wasn't as interested in this, and she kept staring moonily at beautiful Spanish people and saying, *"Buenas noches, buenas noches."* Then, all of a sudden, she said: "Isn't that the racist that stole your watch?"

I looked across the street. A lean, painted man disappeared into the crowd of evening strollers. I started running after him, pushing people aside and darting after the quickly receding figure. People all around me were laughing and yelling, *"Cuidate!"* and *"Perdón!"* annoyed as I ran by. I wasn't even sure Suki had followed, until I became aware of flip-flops smacking behind me and a distinctly American voice yelling, *"Ladrón! Ladrón!"* When the crowd heard that, they started yelling, *"Andale! Andale, Americano!"*

Soon we were off the main drag and back in

the warren of the old town. The streets and the buildings were all made of the same brown stone, and both were narrow and weathered. I would catch a glimpse of the Savage, and then lose him around a corner, catch a glimpse, and lose him again. All of a sudden we were out on the Paseo Maritimo, and the Savage was gone. Suki came up behind me, breathing heavily.

"Where'd he go?"

"That way?"

So we trotted east, trying to keep an eye out but not sure whether we were going the right way. Suki stopped a man who was wearing an official-looking uniform. I looked around for the Savage, and then back at the man. It was a hotel uniform he was wearing, and the man looked very familiar. He was the concierge of the Miramar.

"*Señor, Señorita,*" he said in a sarcastically hospitable voice. "You must have come back to settle your bill."

Suddenly I couldn't breathe, and I imagined that every one of my internal organs was about to fail one by one.

Suki grabbed my hand and started pulling me away, but then the concierge grabbed my collar and pulled us back. He was stronger than he looked, and we went smacking into each other. He ushered us into the hotel—which, we should have noticed, was right behind us—and brought us over to the counter.

"Let me see. Two 'American-style omelets' at twenty-two euros each. Two continental breakfasts at eighteen euros each. Two bottles of champagne, at fifty euros each. Three minibottles of cognac, at ten euros each. Two crystal champagne glasses, replacement charge, thirty-five euros each."

He looked up at me and paused. I held my breath.

". . . and there seems to be this other little charge. What could this be? Seven hundred and eighty euro at the hotel boutique?"

I looked at Suki and let out a little whimper. She had been fidgeting with the hem of her Prada sundress, and now I feared that she might rip it.

"That comes to thirteen hundred and eighty euros with tax and service charges, please."

Suki leaned over to me and whispered, "Maybe we could offer to wash dishes."

"Our boat's leaving at eight. And I think that's really soon."

"Ahem."

I reached into my pocket and pulled out the remainder of the fifteen hundred Rob had wired me. After I had counted out eight hundred and forty-six euros, I was left with thirty-four euros. This was not good. I handed over the cash.

"*Gracias, señor,*" he said sarcastically.

Suki and I looked at each other with panic-stricken faces, and then she grabbed my hand and we ran out of the Miramar and down the dock like our lives depended on it. Which they pretty much did. I ran faster than I probably have ever, because I knew—and Suki must have known, too, because she was running even faster than I was—that this was our last chance.

I waste time and money

There is nothing more humiliating than running to catch a cab, or a train, or, say, a boat. You get all sweaty and everybody knows you're desperate. Plus, it's sort of counter to my whole theory of it's not cool to need anything that badly. Of course, that sort of humiliation is increased exponentially if, having run and sweated and begged for them to wait for you, you are held in traffic for hours and hours. Or, on the ocean, as it were.

When we reached the ferry, breathing heavy and scared shitless that we would be left behind again, the blasé stewardesses took our tickets and ushered us on. It was a big, modern boat, with several levels and a bar, and I promptly wasted a heaven-sent twenty euros that I found in my pocket on gin and tonics for us.

We settled into our seats and looked out at Palma with all its busy streets and the night just about to begin, and agreed that we almost regretted leaving it. Then a few hours passed, and we still hadn't moved. Nobody seemed particularly restless for what seemed like a really long time, and I got very agitated and Suki could tell, so she suggested that maybe it was a Spanish tradition to wait two hours in the dock and that I should lighten up.

Eventually Suki went up and talked to one of the stewardesses, who was drinking red wine and smoking and looking very bored over by the bar. When she came back, she said:

"Well, you'll never guess what. The boat's captain has been invited to dinner at the Spanish royal family's Mallorcan residence, and the boat won't be leaving until they dismiss him."

"Oh."

Then we decided it would be a good idea to combine the very last of our euros and spend it all on more gin and tonics, which we did. I don't know how the hours passed, but they did, and eventually I made myself stop praying that, somehow, the *Ariadne* would be delayed as well, and fell asleep. When I woke up it was the dead of night, and the ferry was moving. Suki was sleeping next to me, her head rested on my shoulder. I looked out at the endless dark sky, and the endless dark water, and wondered how we were ever going to get home. An austere, rocky little island came into my view for a few minutes, and then it was gone.

Arno does it for himself

"Wildenburger!"

Arno staggered to his feet. He had spent the night in one of the very dark, very small lower level detention cabins. When the door opened, the light was almost unbearable. He blinked several times, and then began to make out the face of Barker.

"Wildenburger, I've contacted your parents and informed them that you won't be completing the voyage with us. They are a most valuable client, but I'm afraid your behavior has been reprehensible."

Arno nodded and shifted on his feet. He hoped he could just be out of there soon.

"Stephanie will escort you to the dock," Barker continued, "while I inform Pardo of his situation. There is a car waiting to take you to the Barcelona airport, where your parents have arranged for a flight back to New York."

Barker turned and strode down the hall. Stephanie appeared, smiling apologetically at Arno. She was wearing the same cutoffs she always wore, and an oversize sweater that did nothing to disguise the size of her breasts. Her hair was down, and she looked pretty, like she'd made herself up in a new way or something. She put her arm around his waist and led him away from the cabin.

"Your parents weren't really that mad," she said. "I could tell, because Barker was still angry after he talked to them. Usually, when the parents grovel he's really nice afterward and feels good about kicking bad students off the trip."

"Yeah, whatever," Arno said. "That guy needs to get over himself."

"Uh-huh. He couldn't even get ahold of Mickey's folks, which would usually mean that he couldn't kick Mickey off the boat. Legal issues, you know. But he talked to someone named Caselli? Who, like, basically claimed to be Mickey's caretaker. So that made him *extra* mad, that he didn't even get to yell at an actual parent."

Arno made a sound of disgust. Caselli was Ricardo Pardo's studio manager, and he *was* sort of like Mickey's caretaker. He didn't go easy on him, but he probably wouldn't bust him, either. This reminded Arno, unpleasantly, of how pissed he was at Mickey.

"I think Patch is really going to miss you," Stephanie

said as they stood waiting for Barker to arrive. He looked at her, because he wasn't sure why she'd said that. He caught a whisper of a smile, before she continued, "I mean, he's probably going to feel really *alone*."

"Oh, yeah?" Arno said suspiciously. "Well, he's still got Jonathan."

"Oh, *Jonathan*," she twittered. "Yes, let's hope he gets out of bed sometime in the next five days."

One of the other faculty members appeared with Mickey's and Arno's luggage. Then Barker appeared, with Mickey behind him. Arno gave him a long, cold stare. Mickey stared right back, and Arno could see he that hadn't slept all night and was probably still sort of drunk on anger.

"Pardo, Wildenburger, you two have been a great disappointment to me," Barker said. "Now take your things and go."

Arno grabbed his bag and put it over his shoulder. He walked down the plank without looking back. But he heard Mickey, sure enough, coming along behind. When he got to the dock, he saw the black car waiting.

He looked at Mickey and said, "You can have it. I wouldn't ride with you anyway—you'd probably just fuck everything up." Then he turned and walked quickly down the dock and into the city.

"See ya!" he heard Mickey yell after him. Arno made a bitter waving gesture over his shoulder, but didn't bother taking one last look at his friend.

Mickey watched his friend walk off the dock and into the city. He looked like he knew where he was going. Which Mickey was pretty sure he didn't. Mickey flipped him off to his back, and the *Ariadne,* too, for good measure, and then he started kicking the black car that was waiting to take him to the airport. He kept kicking it until the driver got out and started yelling at him. Mickey yelled back, and that made him feel better. Then the driver got back in the car and took off without him.

"Yeah, well, you suck, too!" Mickey yelled, and then he added some stuff in Spanish so that everyone knew he wasn't some spoiled American brat. He picked up his bag and walked into the city without looking back.

For a long time, Mickey walked as though he was in a trance. Getting kicked out of places was pretty familiar to him, but getting kicked out *and* being abandoned by his friends was new. He walked up Las

Ramblas, the big, two-lane boulevard that ran through the center of the old town. There were lots of tourists strolling in the afternoon sun, and they were seriously bumming Mickey out. Too much laughing and kissing. He got on a bus and rode up through the city. He just kept picturing Arno sneering at him during survival test, or Arno not even looking back as he left him on the docks. Mickey got mad all over again, and then he got melancholy.

He must have been lost in his own head for a while, when he felt someone shaking him awake. It was the bus driver, telling him in Spanish that it was the end of the line. Mickey got out and walked through the streets without thinking about a destination or what he should do next. It was a seedy, hilly neighborhood, and Mickey climbed up through the winding alleys of temporary-looking little structures. Eventually he found himself in a park with wide walking paths shrouded in trees. He walked for a long time, and he started feeling calm, and thinking about things, like the way sometimes nature could tame even his wildest instincts. Of course, that hadn't been true on Barker Island, and that reminded Mickey of Arno, and of Greta. And then he realized that in all this time, he hadn't thought about Greta at all. And now that he had, he didn't miss her particularly. Strangely, suddenly, this made him feel better about everything.

Eventually he came out on a wide plaza that had a view of the whole city. There were tourists there from all over, taking pictures of the view. He went over to the edge and looked out. He looked at all the wide boulevards leading down to the sea, and the vision cleared his head somewhat.

Mickey's first thought was that he hated Barcelona. It was the kind of place all his Venezuelan cousins on his mother's side talked about constantly. They all had bodyguards and wanted to be models and never ate and pouted when they didn't get what they wanted, and they all talked about how "Barthe*loh*na" was their favorite city in Europe, except Paris, and that was only because of the clothes.

His second thought was that he was starving.

He dragged his bag out of what must have been the front entrance of the park, and hailed one of the taxis. Once the car was racing through the streets, back toward the old town, Mickey instructed the driver to take him to a good restaurant. On the way, he told him all about how Arno and he had gotten kicked off the boat, in Spanish. The driver dropped Mickey on an empty little street, and Mickey tipped him absurdly.

"Buena suerte!" the driver called as he pulled away.

The restaurant was small and grottolike, and it had sheets of brown paper for tablecloths. It was a little early for dinner, and there were only a few well-dressed Spanish people sitting around and enjoying an after-work bottle of wine. A dark-eyed, lank-limbed waitress appeared.

"Uno?" she asked him. He nodded, and she led him over to a table. There was piano music in the background. Mickey looked at the menu and decided he was really, really starving. When the waitress came back, he ordered a bottle of wine and paella for two.

The waitress laughed and pushed her long shiny hair over her shoulder. She told him that the paella for two was *"para doth perthonas."* Mickey had never heard anyone pronounce Spanish S's like Th's without sounding pretentious, and he was smitten.

"Estoy esperando alguien," Mickey told her.

"Dijiste una *perthona."*

"Lo siento," Mickey said, clasping his hands and pretending to beg for her mercy.

"Okay-ay." She laughed, then disappeared.

The paella for two took a long time, and he had practically finished the bottle of wine before it arrived. More people were coming into the restaurant by then, and the lovely waitress was moving around the tables in a hurry. He grasped at her apron when she passed, and put his hands around his neck like he was dying of thirst. *"Mas . . . vino . . . por favor."*

She laughed and slapped him away. A busboy appeared a few minutes later and uncorked a very superior bottle of wine. Not that Mickey was discriminating about taste right then. A few minutes later, the busboy brought his food. He refilled his glass and tore into the paella.

He watched the waitress work, becoming ever more drunk and smitten. When she came near him again, he called out, *"Cómo te llames?"*

She walked over, looking bemused, and began to pick up the ravages of the paella. *"Donde está tu compañero?"* she asked.

"Se fue," he replied despondently, forgetting his ruse about the paella for two entirely. *"Tu nombre, por favor."*

"Angelina," she said sweetly, and then leaned in and kissed his cheek. Then she went back to work.

Mickey stayed all night drinking and watching Angelina flicker between tables. He watched the dinner crowd come and go. Later, when he was in no shape to check himself into a hotel, Angelina gave him a cup of black coffee and took him back to her place.

Nobody in Barcelona recognizes Arno

"Does anybody speak English in this godforsaken town?" Arno called out. A few backpackers who were begging on the street looked at him briefly before looking away.

He was dehydrated and mad, and to make matters worse, he was definitely lost. He knew some Portuguese and German, because he was half Brazilian and half German, and he could handle himself in French because of all the art and fashion world functions he'd gone to over the years. But Spanish he couldn't understand at all. He'd spent a few hours trying to get to the airport, and he even managed to get into the subway. But he could never figure out which way he was going, and he couldn't figure out how to ask which was the right way, and eventually he got frustrated and gave up.

Now he was in the city again, wandering down the big main drag. There were vendors selling cheap souvenirs, and everybody was walking really slowly, like they had all the time in the world. He called out for

English speakers again, but everyone continued to ignore him. He decided to take a different tack.

"I need a translator. Anyone? Ten euro for an hour as my trans-la-tor."

He crossed his arms and waited. It took about five seconds for a scrawny kid to emerge from one of the vendor tables and run up to him.

"Good day, sir! Pablo at your service," he said with a little bow. He looked about eleven, and he spoke English with an accent that was both Spanish and British, which Arno had to admit was cool.

"Hey. So I need some help checking into a hotel, and that's it, okay?"

"You need help finding hotel?"

"Yeah, and getting into a room. Does ten euros sound fair?"

"For twenty I will find you the best hotel room in Barcelona."

"Whatever, fine. Pablo, I'm Arno." Arno gave the kid a twenty, and then followed him as he hurried through the busy street. Every hotel they passed, the kid would look up, consider it and shake his head. Finally they came to a big old-fashioned hotel with wrought-iron work across the façade.

"The Hotel Imperial is very good," Pablo said with a grin.

"Looks great. Let's go."

"Wait, Señor Arno. They are very picky at the Imperial. I go first, and get you a room."

"Why would they give you better service than me?" Arno asked incredulously. He had four major credit cards, and he was cleaner than anyone else in this city his age. He couldn't imagine why any hotel in the world wouldn't want to take his money. He didn't want to say that to the kid, though.

Pablo cleared his throat and leaned in to Arno. "I did not want to tell you, but there is much anti-American sentiment in Spain right now."

"Fine. I'll wait here."

The kid nodded deferentially and ran into the hotel. He appeared several minutes later, looking very pleased with himself.

"They have a very good room waiting for you. I will need fifty euros to get the key."

"Oh, come on. They're going to know it's me anyway once I go into my room."

"Señor Arno, I think it is very bad to upset them before we have the key. All the hotel rooms in town are full, it is very lucky that this one is still open."

"Fine, whatever. But come right back." Arno handed over fifty euros, and watched the kid scamper back into the hotel.

While he waited, he wondered if fifty euros could be right. The hotel actually looked sort of high end, and the guests who went in and out looked older and like they had good taste. He watched the hotel door carefully to make sure the kid didn't go in or out. After fifteen minutes, he got totally furious and stormed into the Imperial.

He went right up to the reception desk, but before he could say anything, the girl sitting behind it put her hand up and said, *"El hotel esta lleno."*

"What? Look, have you seen a little kid?"

"A . . . kid?" The girl looked confused, although she clearly understood English.

"Yeah, Pablo, short, scrawny. He was supposed to get me a room."

The girl shook her head.

Arno cursed under his breath, pushed his hair away from his face, and said, "You haven't seen him? Fine. Can I just get a room, then?"

"Sir," the girl said firmly, "the hotel is *full*."

"Fuck!" As Arno cursed, loudly this time, he kicked the desk. The huge vase of flowers sitting on top of it shook, and then fell forward, smashing on the ground. It made a big shattering noise, and pieces of glass sprayed everywhere. Arno jumped back from it, a little stunned, and saw that the girl was in shock, too. She looked like she was going to begin tearing up.

Then he felt the big hands of a security guard on his shoulders, and he was thrown out onto the street. The guy was yelling in Spanish, but when it became clear that Arno didn't understand a word he was saying, he gave up and went inside.

Arno stood alone in the bright sunlight. He put his cop shades back on and walked quickly away from the Hotel Imperial. He was pissed and embarrassed, and pretty much the only thing he could think to do was to find Pablo and make Pablo feel as bad as he felt now.

Suki reminds me of our many differences

Suki hadn't said anything for a while. She was sitting across from me, wearing her big, cheap, Jackie O knockoff sunglasses, and smoking Gitanes. We were sitting at one of the outdoor cafés along Barcelona's main strip that ran up from the dock, and we were both nursing the tiny coffees that our waiter had served us. I hadn't said anything for a long time, either.

Our ferry had come into the port of Barcelona a few hours ago. As it sailed into dock, we watched the *Ariadne* move back out to sea.

We came down the plank way and stared at it for a while. I guess I must have really believed we were going to get back on the *Ariadne*, because I'd spent all our money on gin and tonics and now we were penniless again. Or, technically, just without money, because I *did* have a lot of change in my pocket. When I told Suki that, she got sort of excited and pointed out that the coins were actually like dollars here. We counted out a few one- and two-euro pieces, and then she asked if I would buy her some cigarettes, and then we got into sort of an altercation because I felt like in this sort of dire situation, smoking was *not* a necessity. Then some sleazy Spanish dude who reminded me a lot of Rob, except taller and possibly better looking, interrupted us to make some grandiose speech about how Americans don't appreciate the beauty of life, and by extension, smoking, and then he gave Suki the rest of his cigarettes. Thus the Gitanes.

Suki seemed very pleased with herself after that, and suggested we have coffee and think about our situation. Which pretty much brings us up to speed. We were trying to be very spare with our money, which was hard because coffee in Europe comes in very petite portions and because we had had gin and tonics for dinner last night and both of us probably would have liked to eat something.

The tables were packed close together, and there seemed to be a lot of people out at five on a Wednesday afternoon. I felt like a lot of them were staring at me, but I'm used to that because everyone always stares at me and my friends.

Suki lit another Gitane, and then her eyes got all lightbulblike.

"Hey, you know what? We never got the rest of the money out of my checking account."

I tried not to look at her cross-eyed. "Are you kidding?"

"No . . . I don't really know how much is in there, though. Maybe sixty dollars? And, with the exchange rate, who knows. I mean, it's not going to get us back on the boat. But it might get us a hotel room for the night."

"Hey, Suki? I don't think we're getting back on the boat." I had been thinking about this all morning, and now, since I was feeling pretty brutal, I decided to be brutally honest. There was no way we were going to get ourselves through a foreign country and find a boat that was actually moving fast. Additionally, I didn't want to anymore. My one thought was getting back to New York, and Flan.

"I guess you're right," Suki said, even though she knew nothing of my Flan urgency.

"I think the best thing for us to do is try to make it to my dad's house in London," I said very levelly. "If he's there, he'll get us back to the States."

"How are we going to get to London?"

"Can we think about that tomorrow?"

"Okay."

We paid our bill in coins—which felt really strange—and went off to find a hotel room.

Suki had been to Barcelona on a family vacation, and she seemed to remember it pretty well. We were in the old town, and the street we were on, which was wide and had a big promenade in the center with lots of cafés and tall trees, was called Las Ramblas. Supposedly there were lots of cheap hotels in the little streets that ran off of it. In addition to all the Spanish people who seemed to be lazing about in the late afternoon, there were lots of backpackers, with dreadlocks and mangy-looking dogs, sitting on the sidewalks or walking around. It was sort of like the kids on Saint Marks in the East Village, except these kids really looked like they hadn't been home in years.

We got lost again, of course. Barcelona looked a lot like Palma on Mallorca had, with ancient stone streets that twisted and turned illogically, and nineteenth-century apartment buildings built close together. It was more dirty and urban, though. The shutters all looked bolted down, and when we took a wrong turn, which was pretty much all we were doing, the corner we turned into more than likely smelled like piss.

There were hotels everywhere, but every time we walked into one the clerk looked at us and made an ominous hand gesture and said, *"Lleno! Lleno."*

Eventually, when I was near the point of despair and convinced that my loafers were close to shoe death, Suki clapped her hands and shouted, "Yes!" I looked up at a thin, crumbling building with a really old sign that read HOSTEL LA CUCARACHA. I stared in disbelief, but Suki obviously felt good about it, so I followed her in and up to the second floor.

A tired-looking woman, who looked suspiciously like the clerk at the Mallorca Cucaracha, looked up at us as we came in. Suki smiled broadly.

Suki conferred with the clerk, and then told me that there was good news and bad news. Miraculously they had one room left and they did take cards. The room was fifty-five euros, though, and Suki was worried that her bank would reject the charge.

"What's the worst that can happen?" I asked.

"I'd just be surprised if I have enough with the

exchange rate, that's all."

She handed over her debit card, and after a few tense moments it cleared. The woman gave us the key, and we climbed up the rickety old stairs to our room. I don't need to tell you what the room looked like—it was the same icky kind of room we stayed at in Mallorca. We lay down in the sandpaper blankets, and pretty soon we were sleeping.

I slept for a long time, and I dreamt of an endless succession of holiday parties in a snow white New York with Flan on my arm. She was wearing her clingy red sweater, and her white wool circle skirt, and her cheeks were all pink from eggnog and she smelled like sugar and spice and . . .

Arno at the edge

Arno had been sitting at the outdoor café for at least an hour, and none of the busy waiters had noticed him. They all wore black pants and long white aprons, and they looked perfectly efficient. But still, none of them had noticed Arno sitting there by himself. It was the exact opposite of New York, where everybody paid attention to him and were usually so stunned by his beauty that they also bought him things.

Nobody had bought him anything here. The cathedrals were all ringing seven o'clock, and he wanted food more than anything, and a cold beer to wash it down, and he was ready to pay for it. But he couldn't get the waiters to look at him. After an afternoon of wandering the filthy, foreign streets of Barcelona looking for that little thief Pablo, Arno had told himself that things couldn't get much worse than they already were. But, of course, he had been proven wrong.

Finally, Arno was so angry at the waiters for not serving him that he got up and left.

Earlier, when he had been searching for Pablo, he had passed a place called Hostel La Cucaracha. It didn't look nice (in fact, it looked kind of seedy), but he had the general sense that a hostel was where American kids backpacking through Europe went. Arno used his last little bit of clarity to conclude that the people who worked at such a place might speak American pretty well.

When he climbed the stairs to the second-floor lobby he saw a very cranky-looking woman sitting behind a desk. She didn't even look at him, she just said, *"El hotel está lleno."* Arno recognized that phrase from the Imperial, and it didn't bode well.

"I want a room," he said plaintively.

"Is full," the clerk said.

"Please," Arno said. He was feeling really desperate. "A couch, anything?"

"Out!" she said.

Arno nearly fell down the stairs, humiliated again and hoping she wouldn't remember his face and tell anyone. He went out into the street, where night had fallen, and stumbled down in the direction of the dock where he had left Mickey that morning. When he got there, he smelled the ocean and it reminded him of Barker Island and how angry he had been at Mickey, and how cute Greta was, sort of. He looked at all the happy people taking their evening stroll, and he hated them.

"Mickey!" he yelled at no one in particular. "Mickey, help me! I'm sorry." The strollers backed away from him and went in the other direction. Arno saw a man selling beers out of a cooler on the dock, and walked over. He held up his index and middle fingers, to indicate that he wanted two beers. The man smiled at him, and Arno saw that he had no teeth. *I'm going to end up like this guy,* Arno thought *I'm never getting out of here.* He took the beers, threw a twenty euro note at the guy, and hurried away without waiting for his change.

He staggered off the docks and down the beach, dragging his bag behind him. As he walked, he chugged one beer and then the other, throwing the empty bottles behind him. He kept on as long as he could, calling out Mickey's name, until he was too hoarse and exhausted to go any farther. Then he collapsed on top of his bag.

Patch is the last man standing

"Hey," Patch said to Greta, who had come up behind him but hadn't really surprised him. He hadn't seen her all day, but he'd had a feeling she'd be back around. He hadn't talked to anyone since that morning, when the *Ariadne* had left Barcelona without his friends.

"Hey," she said quietly, passing him a warm mug. She was holding one, too. "It's whiskey with honey and lemon."

The weather had turned soon after they left Barcelona, and they were both wearing sweaters.

"Thanks. Where'd you get it?"

"Barker gave it to me. He said he thought it was probably okay, since I was sick. He said I should bring you one, too."

"Oh. Are you sick?"

Greta gave him a quizzical look and said, "Haven't you noticed that I haven't been around since yesterday morning?"

"Yeah, of course . . ."

"I was in the nurse's office, and then in my cabin with a fever. I guess that survival test did me in."

"Oh. That's too bad. At least you won't be missing any day trips."

After Mickey and Arno's fight, Barker had made an announcement curtailing most day trips and restricting Ocean Term's activities to onboard classes, talks, and recreation. Which was probably a good thing since the weather report said it would be raining in most of their destinations. There was only a light mist now, though. They both looked out at the dark ocean and sipped their drinks.

"I guess we really fucked up, huh?" Greta said after a while.

"Yeah . . . I mean, no, you didn't. But I feel pretty stupid. I mean, I ended up being Barker's pet, which I never planned to be. And now everybody has this idea of me that's totally false."

"I don't think you care very much what everybody thinks of you," Greta said shyly.

"I guess. All I wanted was to see cool places and hang out with my friends, and now all my friends are lost. I guess you call that ironic. I'm usually the one who's out of touch and can't be found."

"Maybe you like it that way."

Patch stopped talking because he always felt uncomfortable when conversations dwelled on him this way.

"Anyway, I'm sorry I didn't know you were sick. I could have brought you flowers or something if we weren't stuck on this boat." He took a sip of his drink and added, "If Mickey or Arno were still on board, they probably would have figured out a way."

"Hey, I know those guys are your friends, but they're kind of assholes."

Patch laughed. "I know. They just *liked* you . . . and Suki."

Greta laughed awkwardly, and then paused like she was thinking out how to say something in her head. "Yeah. I mean, they're cute, but they're dicks, too. That's why . . ."

She stopped talking, and Patch almost felt bad for her, she looked so uncomfortable.

"That's why what?"

"Oh, it's too embarrassing." Greta covered her face with her hands. They were fair and pinkish like the rest of her.

"Hey. Those guys aren't dicks, and neither am I. Whatever it is, it can't be *that* embarrassing."

"Well, that's why I told everybody I had a boyfriend. Because I didn't want to have to deal with all *that* . . ." She giggled awkwardly, then continued talking at a rapid pace. "And that probably sounds really dorky. I mean, I'm sure they weren't even that into me anyway. Guys usually like Suki, and . . . But I'm sort of shy, you know what I mean, and . . . protective of myself . . .and . . ."

Patch looked at her in amazement. She was so awkward and spilling over with feeling, like a skittish kitten. It made him want to be very close to her. He put his hand over her mouth, and he could feel her cheeks heating up against his palm.

"You don't have a boyfriend?"

She shook her head, her lips grazing his palm. So he wrapped her up in his sweatered arms and kissed her. She was warm and smelled clean, almost like baby powder, and he pressed her up against him and kept on kissing her for a long time.

They were only interrupted once, briefly, by Sara-Beth Benny, who was walking by with that guy Loki, Arno's RA. They looked pretty friendly.

"Hey, cuties," she said, laughing as she walked by and winking heavily. She was wearing a fur that looked like some small animal thrown over her small shoulders. Her eyes were bright and she leaned on Loki as they walked by. "Oh, *psstt*, by the way, Patch," she said, lowering her voice as though that alone would prevent Loki or Greta from hearing, "Stephanie's been, you know, looking for you."

Mickey in Bohemia

Mickey's night at Angelina's restaurant turned into a very late night and then a morning at Angelina's place. She lived with her boyfriend, Eduardo, in a huge, ornate house down a little street in the old town. It had been designed by a famous architect and it was all mirrors and dark wood and baroque detail inside. All their friends lived with them, and none of them seemed to work much. In fact, Angelina, whose parents owned the house and seemed to have a lot of money, was the only one with an actual job. Besides Eduardo, who was her family's accountant.

When she and Mickey arrived, there were people lounging around the haremlike central room and smoking pot. Angelina didn't bother to make introductions, she just moved into the most visible seat in the room, made herself comfortable, and sat Mickey down beside her. She put his head in her lap and began to rub it as though it were a crystal ball. Mickey wondered which of the many guys in the room was Eduardo, but he couldn't figure it out. Angelina told everyone the story of how Mickey had finished the paella for two by himself, and all her friends laughed. They were beautiful and smoked a lot and stayed up late every night and made grand statements about art and death that Mickey thought were kind of stupid. He liked being one of them, though. It was like a twenty-four-hour party back in New York. It was like something that might happen at Patch's house.

"Ey, what did you say your name was?" a guy in spectacles asked Mickey. The guy was dressed like a nineteenth-century revolutionary, and his clothes were paint-spattered.

Mickey looked at him blearily and thought to say that he hadn't said what his name was at all. He couldn't quite get that out, though, so he just said, "Mickey Pardo."

"You bear a resemblance to the famous sculptor Ricardo Pardo, *verdad*?"

Mickey sighed. This was the *last* thing he wanted to talk about. "He's my dad."

Everyone got very excited and chattered about how Mickey was the son of a famous artist. They asked him his opinion on a whole range of topics, and pestered him for details of his father's genius. Then they all seemed to collectively forget, and began chattering about something else.

Hours passed like that, and pretty soon Mickey wasn't sure if it was day or night. It seemed a long time ago that he and Arno had split up on the docks, and that made him kind of sad.

"Don't you ever go outside?" Mickey murmured to Angelina, in English this time.

"You want to go outside?" she asked him. Then she clapped her hands grandly. *"Vamos afuera!"*

David tries out a little passive aggression

From: grobman@hotmail.com
To: jonathanm@gissing.edu

Hey man. I haven't heard from you in a few days, so I hope you're OK over there. Rob told me that he wired you a lot of money, so you're probably doing fine and having fun which is cool. I had tea with Amanda the other day. She cried a lot, but I think I might finally be over it. I mean, she's sort of boring, once you get to know her and the mystique is gone, you know what I mean? You'd be proud of me man: I totally don't even care anymore. Oh, and I went to a show at CBGB's with this friend of Feb's called Caroline. Not sure I'm really into her though, she's a little gruff, you know? Been playing a lot of ball, yada yada. Anyway, about what you asked me about Flan and everything, I haven't seen Rob in a couple days, actually since the night you talked to him, so I wouldn't worry. I'm still watching Flan like you asked me to though, so don't worry about that. Just a question though, I thought you sort of tried to break up with Flan before we left. So why are you so worried about her and Rob or really, her and anybody? See you, David.

The Savage won't leave me alone

I woke up feeling really great. But that was before I opened my eyes, of course, and once I made that mistake, I remembered that I was in a smelly room with linoleum floors. I still had a taste of my dream of Flan, though, and that felt good, and also gave me resolve to get the hell out of here. Suki wasn't in the room, either, and that was a relief. Waking up next to her over and over was making feel a little tawdry somehow.

I got myself together and went downstairs. I took my bag with me, just in case—this place was probably full of thieves. Someone was playing guitar in the second-floor lounge, and when I got there I saw that Suki was chilling with a lot of dirty backpackers. There were about five guys, four of them with dreads and layers of weathered clothes, and the other blond and pretty clean-cut. They were drinking espresso from the automatic espresso machine and smoking, again. She didn't notice me, so I slipped downstairs and tried to put a collect call through to my house, but nobody picked up, so I tried Flan's again, but nobody picked up there, either. So I went back upstairs and stood in the doorway until Suki looked up at me.

"Isn't it a little bit early for smoking?"

"Oh, that's my friend Jonathan," she said blandly.

The guys sort of half waved.

"I'm glad you're up," she said. "I had to return the key, since we don't have enough money to stay another night, and we were supposed to be out of the room by eleven. It's twenty of noon, you know."

"Great," I said sarcastically.

"Um, yeah." Suki matched my sarcasm, and then glared at me.

"Well, I just tried my mom and stepbrother and they're not picking up. So I don't know what to do, except go check my e-mail and see if my stepbrother sent a number where my mom can be reached."

"Fine," Suki said with a little impatient cough. She stood up and went around in a circle kissing everyone on both cheeks and saying good-bye in

Spanish. Every time she did this, she leaned over and stuck her butt up in the air in my direction. It was too pathetic for me to watch. When she got to the last—the one blond guy, I think it was—I heard her smacking the two kisses, and then she made this little murmuring noise that made my stomach turn. Why would she put on this show for me? He said good-bye in American-accented English, and he told her to take the rest of his cigarettes with her. When we were outside, she said, "The guys said the Internet café was on Las Ramblas, about four blocks down."

"'The guys'?"

Suki smiled. "Are you jealous?"

"Yeah, right." I had to laugh at that one.

Outside, I realized that Suki was right. It was past noon. The whole city was out, sitting at the cafés and strolling slowly. It was a lovely, breezy kind of day without a cloud in the sky. We found the Internet place pretty easily. It was about the cleanest place I'd been to in all of Spain. It was all chrome and white walls, and I happily used the last of my coins to get us some time on the computers.

My heart fluttered a little bit as my e-mail account opened up, but there was nothing from

Flan. There was nothing from Rob, either, which was both annoying and confusing. A) If he really felt all brotherly with me, how had he not found time to e-mail me my mom's number at Canyon Ranch? and B) Why had he even pretended to be buddies with me in the first place? We were so obviously not. There was one e-mail from David, which basically said nothing except sort of question my interest in Flan, which was definitely not what I wanted to hear from David. Was he on Rob's side or what?

Suki was typing away next to me, and smiling to herself, which seemed inappropriate, so I looked back at the screen and tried to think of something else I could do. I looked at my ghostly reflection in the screen—very gaunt, very Lower East Side. I didn't even look like myself. Which was when I started thinking of the guy Suki had made little murmuring noises at not long ago. And as I thought about his gaunt, snarky face I realized I'd seen it before.

"Oh, my God, what was that guy's name?"

"Which guy?"

"The blond guy you slobbered on this morning."

"Watch it."

"You know who I'm talking about."

"I dunno, Tony, I think he said. I didn't slobber on him, he just bought me an espresso and bummed me a few cigs."

"Tony? Like . . . *Anthony*? As in, *Rhett Anthony Turner.* Oh, my God. You know who that was!?"

"Who?"

"The Savage."

"No."

"I mean, he wasn't a Savage this morning. But that was the Savage."

"Oh, my God." Suki looked genuinely upset. I almost felt bad about the slobbering comment. "And you know what his initials spell?"

We looked at each other and said "Rat" at the same time. "How appropriate," I added.

We ran out of the Internet café and back to the hostel. When we got back to the lounge, we saw the four dreads sitting around. Suki talked to them in Spanish for a minute.

"They say they don't know who he is or where he went," she told me.

We went into the reception area and I went up to the clerk. "Have you seen a Savage?"

"*Cómo?*"

"A Savage. But he doesn't look like a Savage

now. A tall—"

Suki interrupted me to explain to the woman. But she just shook her head.

So for about half a day we ran around the city looking for him until we were exhausted and sweaty and panting and in a complete state of despair.

We were on the dock at this point and the sky was turning rosy as the sun went low over the buildings behind us. On the other side of the dock, the beach began and it ran north along the edge of the city as far as I could see. Suki was looking at it, too, and eventually she said, "We might as well walk down there and find a nice place to rest. Because we got zero dollars, and there's no way we're getting another hotel room for the night."

If Patch checked his e-mail, this is what he would find . . .

From: grobman@hotmail.com
To: patch-o@hotmail.com

Hey man. This is weird, me sending you an e-mail, huh? Anyway, I went shopping with your sisters on Ludlow Street yesterday. Did you know that a pair of girl's jeans goes for more than $100 these days? Apparently, we're talking a pretty average everyday pair of jeans here, according to Feb. Can you believe that? Oh, and I saw Selina Trieff, too. She was walking around with that girl Liesel who Arno used to be with and I don't think she recognized me. Selina wanted to know where you'd disappeared to. How's life on the open seas treating you? Miss you dude, send me a shout out when you get a chance. David.

Patch experiences one of those awkward
moments people keep telling him about

"Pa-atch," a voice came through the door, "are you there, handsome?"

Patch shot up in bed and looked around him. His hair was roughed up in a million directions, and he wasn't wearing a shirt. It was past noon.

"Hold on," he yelled, and looked around for a shirt.

"Pa-atch, where have you bee-en?" singsonged the voice. "I *missed* you."

Patch found a rumpled white T-shirt on the floor and pulled it over his long, tan torso. He seemed to still be getting taller every day, and he had that long, lean skater look to him. He smelled himself before he went to the door to make sure he didn't smell too incriminating. Which he did. He pulled open the door, and saw Stephanie standing there with a big bunch of flowers and a huge, toothy smile. "Where've you been?" she whined flirtingly.

"Um . . ."

"Can I come in?" she asked, pushing past him. "I mean, this whole canceling of day trips is a bummer, but I think it'll give us some time to hang around . . . *in bed,* and . . . Oh, I . . ." Stephanie stopped talking when she saw Greta pulling Patch's sheets over herself. "Hi, Greta," she said, sounding a little stunned and a lot confused. Greta's hair was messed up, too. It was definitely bed hair.

"Hi, Stephanie," Greta said.

Stephanie looked at Patch for an explanation. He shrugged.

"Patch, can you explain to me *why* . . . ," Stephanie began, her mouth hanging open in disbelief.

"Um, Steph—"

"I mean, what is that *little girl* doing in your *bed!*"

"I think you better go."

Something broke across Stephanie's face right then, like she might cry. She threw the bouquet of flowers at Greta. They hit the wall behind her, and then broke apart and fell around her on the blankets.

"Oh, no you don't!" Stephanie shrieked. "Don't think you can just dog *me.* There are rules against this sort of thing, you know. Any girl found sleeping in a boy's cabin or vice versa will be kicked off the ship, and this looks pretty goddamned incriminating to me. I'm gonna send you where all your friends went, except somewhere worse. *Way* worse."

"Steph," Patch said. He was frustrated, but not quite worried yet.

"Don't *Steph* me. We're over, we're over!"

"Um, I don't think, technically, we were ever together . . ."

"Oh, yeah? Pack your shit! You're out of here!"

"Ms. Rayder?" They both turned and looked at Greta. She had stood up, and she was wrapped in a sheet with her reddish hair falling down her back. A few pale pink roses fell off the bed as she stepped toward them. She held up a card that she had taken from the bouquet. "This might be a teensy-weensy bit more incriminating. You want me to read? Okay. 'Dear Patch. I've really enjoyed the blossoming of our friendship, and now I know I want my flower to blossom for you. Let's have an early Valentine's. Be mine, xo Stephanie.'" Greta giggled. "Incriminating, *and* cheesy."

Stephanie stamped her foot and put her arms over her big chest. She looked either like she was about to start spitting flame or pouting.

"I think you'd better go," Patch said.

"Well . . ." Stephanie's lips were trembling as she attempted some kind of last word. "Well . . . neither of you can expect any college recommendations from *me*!"

She fled the room, slamming the door behind her.

Patch looked at Greta and smiled. The sun coming through the porthole lit up her hair in this really beautiful way. He moved toward her and pulled her down into the sheets with him. They rolled around and got hopelessly twisted up and burst out laughing.

"You, I'm not letting go of," Patch said, and then he smiled.

A heart-wrenching beachside reunion

Angelina and her friends wound their way through the city like a charmed circus troupe, with Angelina as the leader. She carried a white parasol, and as she walked she rested her arm around Mickey's shoulder. The rest of the group were dressed in their flowing, colorful bohemian threads, and they carried picnic baskets and blankets and big umbrellas. When they reached the beach, they walked along it for a long time, until they found a relatively uninhabited place, and then they set up. Everyone smoked up, and then Mickey ran around entertaining them with cartwheels and back-flips.

One guy had brought a guitar, and he started playing an intricate flamencolike tune. A picnic lunch of olives and aged Manchego and red wine was passed around, and Mickey started feeling warm and lazy and good. He squirmed his way in between Isabel and Susana, Angelina's two younger sisters. They looked like mini versions of her, skinny and tan with droopy dark eyes and long hair that fell below their waists.

Other friends came in from the city, and Angelina kissed them three times on the cheek hello and insisted that they meet Mickey. One of them was wearing a huge crown of twigs on his head. Because of the crown, his blond hair, and long, thin features, he looked like Christ.

"That's Rhett," Angelina told Mickey, by way of explanation. "He's a performance artist."

"Oh." Mickey shook the guy's hand, then rested back between Isabel and Susana.

That was when he saw the lone figure, sort of stumbling down the beach. The guy was dragging a suitcase behind him, and his hair was messed up, and he looked like he hadn't had anything to eat or drink in a while. Mickey sat up and called out to him.

The guy looked around blearily and dropped his case. It was definitely Arno, although he looked scrubbier than pretty much ever. Mickey was so happy to see him, he forgot they were fighting at all. He ran over and gave him a rambunctious hug, knocking him to the ground.

"What happened to you? You look like shit!" Mickey yelled even though he was on top of Arno now.

"They threw me out of the hotel I was supposed to stay in, and they stole my money," Arno croaked.

Mickey remembered how angry he had been, but

Arno seemed so pathetic that it was hard to keep it up. He dragged him over to the picnic and introduced him to everybody. The girls immediately pulled Arno down onto the blankets and began feeding him with their hands and combing his hair with their fingers.

Once he was feeling revived, Arno went with Mickey for a walk down to the water.

"How did you find these people?"

Mickey was drawing a blank, so he just said, "Through Angelina."

"She's hot."

Mickey gave him a look.

"Sorry, man," Arno said. He hung his head, and Mickey knew he meant it.

"Yeah, be careful, anyway. She's a big flirt and she's got a boyfriend."

"Oh. Anyway, I can't believe I left you for twenty-four hours and already you have new friends."

Mickey rubbed his eyes. "Twenty-four hours? Is that it? I feel like I've been in that house for days."

"House?"

"Yeah, we'll stay there tonight. And then what do you say we split? I'm digging this whole Barcelona scene. But I feel like if I don't get out soon I'll be stuck here forever, drinking bitter coffee and having serious conversations about flirting or some shit for the rest of my life."

They both laughed. "I feel you. You just get us to the airport, and we can go stay at the Lober-Luccis' in London until our flight back to New York. They're these art dealers that my family has know forever. Sounds like a plan?"

"Sounds awesome."

"And Mickey?"

"Yeah?"

"I really am, you know, sorry."

"Shut up." Mickey put his arm around Arno and they walked back to Angelina's party.

When the sun started going down, they all went back to the house and got very drunk on red wine.

Yeah, I slept on a beach once

Suki and I watched the party at woeful dis-
tance. They were a bunch of hippie types, having
a picnic on a beach, and they all looked like they
were having fun. Plus, they were eating, and at
this point we were pretty hungry. There were two
guys that looked like my friends who came near
us for a few seconds—a tall handsome one and a
short stocky one with a shaved head—and that
made me want to be a part of their fun even
more. The Arno clone was pretty disheveled,
though, and the Mickey one was pretty mellow.
Both things were sort of opposite of the real Arno
and Mickey, so I decided I must be suffering from
hunger delusions, and I kept low until they
started packing up to leave.

When we were sure they were all gone, we ran
down to where they had been sitting and looked
through their scraps. This is something that
really bothers me, and something I hope I never

do again. But for the record, yes, there was a time and place where I went digging through other people's garbage for dinner. And it was a good thing we did, because they had left some cheese and bread and wine and olives, and also a blanket, which we really needed if Suki was serious about sleeping on the beach. Everything had a familiar smell to it, too, which I decided after a while had to be pot.

We dusted the sand off everything and set ourselves up. Then we tore into our salvaged meal, which was actually surprisingly delicious. I have since realized that this was more because I was starving than anything else, but still.

"I wonder who those people were," Suki said wistfully.

"Freaking hippies, from the looks of it."

"Wouldn't you love to live like that someday? I mean, spend all day at the beach playing music and just talking about life."

This is the weird thing about Suki, I was realizing. She could be totally sarcastic and bitchy one minute, and then super hokey the next. I didn't get it, so I just said, "Yeah . . ." kind of slowly.

"I'm sorry that we missed the Savage again," Suki said. "I feel really bad that I didn't recognize him. I know you really want your watch back, but maybe it's better you not get it. Like, maybe it's bad juju or something."

I couldn't believe that she'd used the word "juju," so I just said, as nicely as possible, "It's not like anything good has happened to us while I *haven't* had it."

"That's not entirely true."

"Suki, I don't mean to be rude. But what the fuck are you talking about?"

She smiled her vague little smile, and said, "Oh . . . I'll tell you in a minute. But first, I want to take a swim."

It was dark by now, and the full moon cast a long reflection on the water.

"No way."

"Why not?"

"It's dark."

"So?"

"It's cold."

"It is not."

"Well, I don't want to."

"Oh come on. You would hate for me to be right, wouldn't you? About dudes being the ones who just want to be comfortable and the ladies being the brave ones."

"Okay, it is so not about that."

"What's it about then?"

I sighed, and figured I might as well tell her. I mean, I had just eaten garbage with her—I could probably be a little vulnerable. "You know the trip I took before Ocean Term? The one on my step-mother's yacht—"

She snorted when I said "yacht." I ignored her.

"Well, we were swimming in this little cove near this Venezuelan fishing town. And I swam out really far, and it was really deep, and it felt great. And then I felt this really sharp pain in my leg, and I looked down and I saw this purple blob swimming away. And then I started puffing up and I couldn't breathe and they had to take me to this really filthy hospital in the middle of nowhere . . . that's another story. But I'm not going back in the water. There are *things* out there."

Suki laughed. "Well, I'm going for a swim. And if you don't come with me, I might drown, and then you'll never know my secret."

I paused. "I wish you wouldn't."

"Well, I'm going."

"I'll put my toes in with you. But that's it."

I walked down with her and I rolled my jeans up to my knees. We walked out a little way; the water was shallow and pretty warm from the day of sun. Suki took her dress off and threw it back on shore, and so I did the same with my shirt, since it seemed like if she took something off, I should, too. She waded farther into the water in her underwear, and then she dove under. She didn't come up for a long time, and then I felt two hands around my ankles and before I knew what was happening I was under water. At first I was in total shock, and then I was worried about my jeans. But when I came up for air, Suki had her arms around my neck, and she kissed me. It was a really soft, wet kiss. And even though I should have been thinking only of Flan, touching somebody felt really nice and good after all these days of stress. So I kissed her back, and when she swam away I followed her and we swam around each other for a long time in the moonlight.

When we came out of the water, we toweled off with the big fluffy Miramar towels. We lay down on the blanket and looked up at the sky. The whole city of Barcelona was probably out having a great time behind us, but we didn't care. We looked up at the stars and started telling each other things. We talked for a long time, and when it was really late and we were both sleepy, she asked if I wanted to hear what her surprise was.

"I thought that was it, when you kissed me," I said, leaning over and putting my hand on her stomach.

"Yeah, I guess I have another one."

"Okay, shoot."

"Well, you know how I was really shocked that my card worked at the hostel yesterday?"

"Uh-huh . . ."

"I found out why. When I checked my balance at the Internet café today, I found out that I have this thing called checking plus. It means that I can overdraw my account by five hundred dollars, and not be penalized. Which means that we have a way to get to your dad's house in London!"

I shot up and pulled my hand away from Suki. This was a surprise, and not a very nice one.

"So what are we doing on the beach, then?!"

Suki looked hurt, and she stuck her lower lip out.

"And how stupid are you not to have realized this four days ago?!"

I stood up really pissed. But then that moment passed, and I just felt physically wrecked by all the up and down emotions. It was intense. And then I thought that maybe Suki was right. Maybe

I was trying to be all safe and warm, and what I really needed in my life was someone who surprised me. Everything seemed new right then, like I'd never seen any of it before, and my life could be totally different from this moment on.

So I knelt down, and I told her I was sorry, and I kissed her. And then we started kissing more. It wasn't, like, I've-wanted-this-so-long, now-we're-a-couple kissing. It felt sort of like an experiment, and that seemed okay.

I was on a beach in Spain with a girl who totally pissed me off. We were making out, on a full-moon night, with our toes in the sand, and I felt like a totally different person, and that feeling was really freaking good.

A daring escape

"Pssssttttt!" Arno hissed, trying to be as quiet as possible and still wake up Mickey. The big central room in Angelina's house was filled with ornate couches and chairs and big velvet pillows. There were exotic plants, and really old-looking paintings on the walls. Many of the people he'd met at the picnic the day before had come home with them, and they had fallen asleep right there in the living room, amongst full ashtrays and empty wine bottles. Mickey had fallen asleep with his head in Angelina's lap, and Angelina, who was snoring softly in her sleep, was resting against a big red and gold pillow. Arno shook Mickey until his eyes opened.

"Where are we?" Mickey asked, a little too loudly.

"We're still in Angelina's," Arno whispered back

Mickey bolted up. Angelina stirred in her sleep, but didn't seem to wake up. "We've got to get out of here. I can feel my will crumbling with every passing moment."

"Uh, where'd you leave your stuff?" Arno laughed.

"Can't remember."

"Think."

"Maybe by the front door?"

They went to the foyer, which was cluttered with coats and shoes and umbrellas and unopened mail. One of the partygoers from yesterday was sprawled across the bench in the foyer.

"There it is!" Mickey said triumphantly. The sleeping guy's feet were resting on his bag.

"Hey, isn't that the performance artist?" Arno said with a hint of derision in his voice.

"Whatever," Mickey said as he stealthily lifted the guy's legs and extracted his bag.

"How do you think a performance artist got a watch like that?"

They both looked closer. "I don't know, maybe they're *all* rich."

"Isn't that Tiffany? The kind of watch Jonathan wears?"

"Weird."

"Very weird," Arno said. He leaned over and slipped it off the sleeping guy's wrist.

"Yo. These people have been nice to us."

"So? And besides, *this* guy hasn't."

"It's not Jonathan's watch. It's just one like his."

"How do you know? Jonathan is lost out there somewhere, too."

"Fine." Mickey could feel a fight coming on, and he was feeling weirdly peaceful. They grabbed their luggage and stepped outside, shutting the door very quietly behind them.

Outside, the city was just waking up. They walked sleepily out onto the main drag. The street cleaners were coming through, hosing away all the debris of last night's party. The bread trucks were making their deliveries, and the waiters from the outdoor cafés, in their long white aprons, were setting up the tables for breakfast.

"*Taxi!*" Mickey yelled, and one of the passing little white cars shrieked to a halt.

"It's the same in Spanish?" Arno groaned, remembering his own difficulties yesterday.

"Yeah. Except you say it kind of different." Mickey said. When he got in, he instructed the driver in Spanish to take them to the airport. They both stared out the window as they left the old city for the broad avenues of Barcelona proper. Arno was very relieved not to be stuck alone in a foreign city anymore. And he could tell by how quiet and introspective Mickey was being that he felt that way, too.

I get all nostalgic for something I never had

"Ta-da!" Suki cried, throwing her arms up as she emerged from the weird train station ladies' room.

We had about an hour to kill before the 11:00 train that would take us from Barcelona to Paris, where we would catch a train to London. I had managed to get my hair pretty much into shape, and my jeans had dried from last night's dip and actually fit better now. I had given up on making myself looking any cleaner, so I had just been waiting out in front of the bathrooms. Suki had somehow emerged from the bathroom looking pressed and rested and delicious in her pink sundress and her braids carefully redone.

"You're bangin'," I said, and kissed her ear.

"Hey, thanks. You aren't bad yourself."

"So, let's get breakfast."

We walked through the train station, which was very modern and cavernous and flooded with mid-morning light. Arrival and departure announcements echoed through the space. There were kids with backpacks sitting on the floor, sleeping or reading tattered paperbacks.

There was a café near the entrance, and we ordered pastries and café con leche. Suki had taken forty euro out from an ATM and bought our train tickets with her bank card. She'd also bought a deck of cards, a pack of Gitanes, and an *International Herald Tribune*, even though I'd reminded her how boring it was when we got it in Mallorca.

We read the paper over each other's shoulders and then played gin. Suki had her big glasses on, and she looked very ladylike while she smoked her cigarettes. The whole scene had the illusion of some remote, glamorous time, when people were ambivalent about everything and drifted from one country to another. Eventually they called our train, and we took our bags and went down to the platform.

We found our seats in one of the second-class cabins. The seats were all little and upholstered with fuzzy red cloth, and the baggage rack above our heads was tarnished brass. Everything felt very retro in there, too. We settled into our seats and Suki put her head on my shoulder. Other passengers came in, and pretty soon the car had fallen silent in anticipation of the trip.

Everyone was very quiet as the train lurched into motion and began speeding out of the station. I thought about Flan, and how my urgency to get back to New York and to her had subsided since last night. I would deal with that when it came, I guess. Outside the window, the city had given way to country and there were hay bales and fields as far as I could see. We would be in Paris soon enough, and then to London, and we would go on to New York from there.

"Do you wish you could go back? For your watch?" Suki asked.

"A little bit. But maybe you're right. Maybe it's bad . . . luck."

Suki laughed and said, "You know what, Jonathan, I think you and I are going to get along famously."

"Yes," I said, "wouldn't it be pretty to think so?"

And with that, Suki snorted at me.

Mickey and Arno do some healing

"Yeah, love you too, Mom," Arno said into the phone, rolling his eyes at Mickey. They were sitting across a tea table in the upstairs drawing room of the Lober-Luccis' London town house. Mickey snickered, then took a very affectedly snooty sip of his tea, slurping it at the last minute. "Yup," Arno was saying, and "Thanks," and "I know it wasn't my fault, Mom. But that means a lot." Finally, he put down the phone and let out a sigh of relief.

"So she let you off the hook?" Mickey asked, shaking his head in mock disapproval.

"Yeah, looks like it." Arno smiled. "I just exaggerated how desperate I was in Barcelona, and her heart went out to me."

"Nice. I wonder if that'll work with mine."

Arno looked at him seriously and said, "You should do it sooner than later. I think our parents are all totally still guilting over . . . you know."

"Nah. You're probably right, but I'm not quite ready

to deal." Mickey picked up one of the tiny watercress sandwiches from the tea table and put it into his mouth. Chewing, he said, "So where are these people?"

"I don't know, man. But let's hope they don't show up. They'll probably just want dirt on my parents if they do."

When Arno had called the Lober-Luccis from the Barcelona airport yesterday morning, they had told him he could absolutely stay with them in London for a few days. After all, the Wildenburgers had known them since the early eighties, when Marianne Lober and Carlo Lucci were just ambitious young things on the London art scene. They had said that they might be in and out to their country estate, however, and also that they had a few little cocktail engagements planned over the next week. "I do hope I get to see you, though, darling . . . ," Marianne Lober-Lucci had said, as she passed the phone to her assistant to give Arno directions to the house.

When they arrived late last night by cab, the head maid ushered them upstairs and drew baths for them and got them settled into one of the upstairs bedrooms. When they went out for a walk the next afternoon (to eat a lunch that consisted largely of beer), she had called cheerily after them, "Don't forget teatime! Mrs. Lucci will be so upset if I don't make your tea." As they walked away, she had added, "If she comes back this evening . . ."

Arno got up and walked about the room. The walls were painted dark red, and there were several impressionist period paintings on the walls. "You want to take a look around the house?"

Mickey followed him out of the drawing room and into the grand hall. They wandered through the private galleries, which were filled with Rembrandts and Titians and other famous artists. When they got to the contemporary gallery, they saw a big, abstract chrome sculpture in the center of the room, lit from above. It looked like a woman bursting out of the ground, sort of. It was an early Ricardo Pardo.

"I think that's one of your dad's," Arno said.

"Yeah, but it must be from a long time ago. He hasn't made anything that looks like that in a long time." Mickey walked around it, looking at the art that hung on the far walls. "Hey, isn't this your fam?"

Arno came over and looked at the canvas Mickey was pointing toward. It was done in a photo-realist style, with bright colors. It showed Arno's father standing behind his mother, whose arm draped protectively over a ten-year-old Arno. They all had placid expressions on their faces, and looked perfectly, beautifully, boringly real. Except that the artist had given them all animal hands: Arno had goat's hooves, and his mother had cat's paws, and his father had hawk's talons. The effect was surreal.

"Leland Morton. I remember sitting for that painting. It was so boring. We had to sit for him every day for weeks, and he was such a perfectionist. It sucked. And we had just met Patch, and you guys were all over at his house playing video games . . ." Arno paused for a long breath, ". . . and I thought you guys had replaced me."

"You do look pissed." Mickey laughed.

Arno laughed, too, and said, "Yeah, I think I was thinking, *Fuck all of them if they leave me behind,* you know?"

"Aw, we'd never do that!"

"I know," Arno said, adding, "Shut up," for good measure.

They heard voices in the hall, and two people carrying martini glasses burst into the room.

"Oh! Arno, you're here!" It was Marianne Lober-Lucci, and a guy who was a lot younger than her husband. Her skin was very tan and tight, and she wore a clingy black long-sleeved dress and lots of gold jewelry. She had that same creepily preserved look that Arno's mother had. She came over and hugged Arno and kissed him on either cheek. "My, aren't you handsome.

And you must be Ricardo Pardo's boy." She kissed Mickey's cheeks, too. "Meet Rafik Merleau, the architect."

The guys all shook hands.

"Thanks for letting us stay, Marianne. It's really gracious of you," Arno said, turning on his full charm.

"Of course, you delicious thing. Now, what are you two doing up here? You must come play with the grown-ups."

As they walked down the back stairs, toward the chatter and noise of an elegant party, Mrs. Lober-Lucci called back, "Get yourselves some drinks, darlings. And then I want to hear all about your parents, Arno Wildenburger."

Arno never responds to e-mail he doesn't understand

From: grobman@hotmail.com
To: arnow@gissing.edu

Yo Arno. Thanks for keeping in touch, man, that's really sweet. Just kidding, things have actually been really cool here. I've been having a lot of fun with Rob and some girls. Anyway, I was wondering if I could get some tips from you, about, you know, girls. I think I have a real crush right now, but I don't want to blow it the way I always do. Ha ha. Anyway, any like pointers on how to keep her interested, but not like overwhelm her, would be appreciated. I'll see you when you're back in NYC, right? Later, David.

The dirt on Barker

The party downstairs was just the sort of under-stated event the Wildenburgers might have thrown in their Chelsea town house. A mix of punky young artists and established, well-dressed art dealers mingled among servers who passed out raw tuna appetizers and fine wine. A piano was tinkling in the next room over. Marianne Lober-Lucci walked Arno and Mickey around the room. Mickey found an out pretty quickly, and wandered the room eating and drinking things. Arno was swept up into the tenth explanation for the party that evening.

"Yes," Marianne was saying, "we love the new gallery Rafik has designed for us. I wonder if you subscribe to the theory that art is better seen in a gallery that is in itself a piece of art rather than in a blank room, as I do."

"Well, it certainly sells better," a man joked. Everybody twittered.

Marianne took Arno's arm and walked him around the room some more.

A crowd had gathered around Mickey, who was holding a beer and gesticulating wildly. He was telling the story of their expulsion from the ship.

"No!" Marianne said, when he was finishing up. "Roger Barker . . . ? Why, Carlo knew him at Oxford. So that's what the old bastard is up to."

"You knew Barker back in the day?" Mickey asked in disbelief.

"Oh, yes, he was always very pretentious and none of us liked him much. He's tried to do all sorts of things, you know, even tried breaking into the art scene for a while. But educational cruises! How *middle*brow. Wait till Carlo hears this. He is absolutely going to *die*."

Everyone laughed and drank some more. Mickey and Arno were forced to tell the story again and again, and it became more extravagant every time, with Barker becoming fatter and more evil with each telling.

Later on, Marianne started recalling the Wildenburgers of the eighties, and then Arno and Mickey drifted away. Someone turned the music louder, and the crowd sort of shifted in age and style. The guys found themselves sitting on a couch, next to an artsy-looking girl wearing a designer dress with big combat boots and a ratty scarf, and another girl who had buckteeth and was dressed very proper, like she had just come from a tennis lesson. She was probably one of the collectors' daughters. They talked about what kids did in London, and then Arno whispered to Mickey, "We're going to have a good time tonight, and tomorrow we are definitely getting on that plane to New York."

"Absolutely."

"And when we get there, we are never leaving Manhattan again."

"Gotcha."

I am *that* close to home

I knocked on the door, fingering my dad's card. When he'd given it to me, I'd thought it was strange and kind of cold for my dad to give me, his kid, his card, even if it was his personal home address one. "You'll always have a home here," he'd said, but that's not really the kind of thing my dad says, so it sounded really forced and cheesy. But I had to admit now that it was a good thing, however weird, because we never would have found the house otherwise. Of course, it was the grandest on the block. I knocked louder.

"I think there's a bell," Suki said after a few minutes. "Right there."

The weather had been steadily declining, and when we reached London we were met by driving rain.

"Oh," I said, feeling more than a little silly. I rang the bell, and a few moments later the door swung back.

The long whiskered face of an old man peered out at us.

"Yes?" he asked in a crisp British accent.

"Is Lady Suttwilley, or her, um, her husband in?" I asked.

"No."

"Oh. Well, I'm sorry we're meeting under these circumstances. But I'm Jonathan, Pl... Lady Suttwilley's new stepson."

The old man looked at me skeptically. He was wearing a plaid vest and very expertly cut black suit pants, and though he had obviously been a tall, lean man when he was younger, he now had a paunch visible beneath the vest. Or possibly accentuated by it. Finally he said, "You don't look like Jonathan."

I looked down at myself. I was a little rumpled. My bag, which at this point was faded from sun and crusted with sand, looked like a backpacker's; my lips were chapped; and my shirt had stretched so that it looked about two sizes too big for me. I guess he meant I didn't look like the Jonathan that had been described to him. And I guess that sort of made me happy. "Yeah, you're right. But I've just spent I don't even know how many days and nights in trains and boats and hostels, and even one night on the beach. I just spent thirty-six hours riding in the second-class car of a slow train that stopped in every village in France. So I don't really look like me at all. But my dad lives here, and I'm pretty sure he'd want me to stay. Even if he did see what I looked like now." I handed the old man my dad's card, and he looked at it.

"You sure you're not one of Monsieur Rob's friends, then?" he asked, arching an already very arched, very gray eyebrow.

"No, not at all," I said quickly. As soon it came out of my mouth, I realized it probably wasn't the tone to take. "I mean, *yes*, I know him a little. From the honeymoon. On Lady Suttwilley's yacht. But we only met like a month ago."

"And mademoiselle, she's not one of Monsieur Rob's friends?"

"No. This is Suki. A . . . friend of mine."

"Very good. I am Lady Suttwilley's butler. Forgive me if I was rude; Monsieur Rob's friends always muck up the house." He ushered us in and shut the door behind us. The front rooms were filled with mirrors and great china vases stuffed with irises. He walked quickly through the opening halls of the house, talking to us over his shoulder. ". . . for some reason, they like to urinate on the family heirlooms. The girls especially. No offense, miss, I knew from the start you weren't one of them."

"Thank you," Suki said happily.

"Now, you both need to get cleaned up. And then we'll feed you. This is actually very well-timed, because I haven't had a thing to do since Lady Suttwilley and your father went away."

"Where are they, exactly . . . ?" I ventured.

The butler stopped and turned slowly around. "Young man," he said impatiently, "I know in your country young people are involved in everything a family does. But in this part of the world we are old-fashioned, and we like to keep some privacy. And for this reason, there are still *some* vestiges of romance. I have served Lady Suttwilley since her first marriage, and I have never once betrayed her hideaway in the Cotswolds."

With that, he turned on his heel, and led us through a complex series of servants' staircases until we arrived in a hallway.

"Now, this is the young monsieur's wing. You can stay in his room while you are here. And you may stay as long as you like, and then I will have an excuse to make my famous welsh rarebit. I hope you like welsh rarebit. Now." He disappeared into a room, and reappeared with two robes. He handed one to each of us. "There is monsieur's room, and next door is a guest room for mademoiselle. Take your time cleaning up. And when you are ready, come down for supper."

He turned and was gone.

"I feel like I'm in a movie." Suki giggled. "You are *so* not related to these people."

"Yeah, I know," I said. "I'm really not."

I get a little peek into my new stepbrother's life

I finished bathing first and I went out into Rob's room. It was eerily like my room, very spare and muted. He had a very tricked-out vinyl setup, and like a million records in a very complicated shelf contraption. His desk had a very different feel, though, polished and antique and really, really expensive. I sat down, and thought I'd try my mom again, just for good measure.

Of course she didn't pick up her cell or our house phone. I thought about calling the Flood house, but I had been feeling so sort of ballsy and come-what-may, I felt like a big, hard talk with Flan right now would just be really misplaced. For a minute I thought about calling David, but his last e-mail seemed so judgmental. And at this point, I just wanted to get home without anyone's help, and I knew if I got in contact with any of my friends, there would be a big rescue mission and everything would go on as before. So I sat at Rob's desk and started going through drawers. For the record, this is never a good idea.

First drawer: boring. Pens, ink cartridges, that sort of thing. Second drawer: nothing I wouldn't have guessed. Lighters, various smoking paraphernalia, probably bought in Amsterdam or some other Eurotrash mecca. Third drawer: (seemingly harmless) a big stack of snapshots. But as I began to go through them I realized that they were all of Rob . . . with girls. Not the same girl, or two or three girls, but lots and lots of different girls. And some of the pictures I wouldn't have felt comfortable showing Flan. And all of a sudden, I was thinking of Flan again. Fourth drawer: underwear, women's, lots of it. Was he, like, some kind of panty thief perv, or had girls just given them to him? And if they had, how does one go about asking for something like that? And then I stopped asking those questions, because the fact was, he was in New York with Flan Flood, and I was in London.

This is why I should never leave Manhattan.

Somebody knocked at the door, so I

slammed the drawer shut and turned around.

"Jonathan," Suki called through the door, "Are you decent?"

"Hold on," I said. I grabbed a T-shirt and jeans out of Rob's closet and put them on. Surprisingly, they fit really well. "Come in."

Suki came in and threw herself down on Rob's bed. She was wearing the sundress from Mallorca, and once again she had somehow gotten it to look clean and wrinkle-free. "This house is unbelievable," she said. "You're like gentry."

"Yeah, that's my dad, not me. But thanks," I said. I was being sarcastic, but Suki didn't seem to notice.

"Anyway, I think that butler guy made us dinner. And I'm starving. You wanna go check it out?"

"Yeah, okay."

As I followed her down the stairs, she called out, "Don't you love that about traveling? You're always starving, and everything always tastes good."

*   *   *

When we finished eating, the butler cleared our plates and sat down with his pipe. He obviously wanted us to stay, but I was itching to find a phone or a computer or something that would get me home to Flan.

"Wine?" he asked. "The young monsieur always has wine with dinner, but you two didn't drink a thing."

"I'd love a glass," Suki said.

I asked for a beer. As he got us our drinks, Suki asked, "Why do you call him monsieur? I mean, you're not French, are you?"

The old man shrugged his shoulders. "He likes it. It took me a long time to grow accustomed to it, of course, and still sometimes I slip up. But it reminds him of his childhood, so I oblige him."

"But isn't he half British and half Venezuelan?" I asked

"Oh, no no. Penelope's second marriage—after Lord Suttwilley, and before Benito Isquierdo—was to Yves de la Tour. Surely you've heard of him?"

We shook our heads.

"Oh. These *are* different times. Well, Rob Tour, as he was known in this country. 'Rob' was a nickname he earned because he would rob your money, and then your women." The old butler chuckled, like that was the funniest thing he had ever heard. "Penelope ran off to the south of France with him, and they conceived the young monsieur and lived there for some time. But old Rob Tour got restless eventually, and he left her his fortune and went off to make another one in some other part of the world. Lord Suttwilley still loved her, the old fool. And he took her back. But he never let her forget where the boy came from. He called him Rob to the day he died, just to torture her."

"Oh, is that how Rob got his nickname?"

"Oh, that and . . . Well, he is his father's child." The butler chuckled again. "It's better than his given name, I suppose. You know they named him after Serge Gainsbourg? Well! I told them not to, but no one ever minds me. Now then, to the study? I made some wonderful cookies this afternoon . . ."

As we followed him through the halls of the house, Suki nudged me, all, like, "Isn't this funny?" But I was feeling pretty low and desperate, so I didn't say anything. In fact, this was

about when I stopped being able to talk to Suki
in full sentences because all I could think about
was Flan and what Rob might or might not be
doing with her panties.

Psychoanalysis for breakfast

It was noon when David woke up and realized that today was the day his friends had been saying they were coming home. He had no idea how he felt about that, and so he decided he should call Rob up and they should go see what Flan and February Flood were up to. They'd hung out with them the last two days in a row, and David had felt more happy and comfortable than he had in a while.

He skidded into the living room in boxers and socks, but he was stopped on his way to the bathroom.

"David," his father said, without turning away from the window. His dad was staring off into space, like he always did for at least half an hour every Sunday morning. He had this theory that ninety percent of what ailed the modern person could be cured by half an hour of quiet contemplation a week, and he was strict with himself. "Something is troubling you."

"Uh . . . not really, Dad."

"Is it . . . about your friends?"

"Um, yeah, probably. But—"

"David, sit down."

David sat down on the ottoman in front of his dad's chair and waited. Sam Grobart kept his eyes on the window.

"What's wrong with your friends?"

"Dad."

"Is it about the trip?"

David had had a lifetime of experience with his dad's analysis. The best thing to do was to give the obvious explanation, and confirm his thinking. "Yeah, well, it feels really unfair that I got kicked out when they're always breaking more rules than I am."

"Mmmm . . ."

"I mean, it's just dumb luck, I guess. But then none of them even bothered to e-mail or call or check up on me or anything. They're probably all having a great time, and they won't even remember my name when they come back."

"Yes. How does that make you feel?"

"Pissed off!" Weirdly, this *was* making David feel better. "And then Jonathan e-mails me, but it's like all he wants to know is how Flan's doing . . ."

"You've been spending a lot of time at the Floods', it seems."

"Yeah, well, Jonathan asked me to 'keep an eye on

her' for him, because he's paranoid that his new step-brother is going to steal her away."

"Mmmmm . . ."

"But actually, hanging out with the three of them has been a blast. It's almost a relief."

"Let me tell you a little story, David. When I was a junior at Yale spending all my time trying to get into the honors thesis class for my senior year, I had a friend. Let's call him . . . John. He was more of a party type, and he always had cute girlfriends. He decided he wanted to take his second semester of his junior year abroad in Spain, and when he left he asked me to keep an eye on his girl du jour, Hilary, for him. Well, when he came back from Spain, Hilary wasn't his girlfriend anymore. I never did get into the honors thesis class, but that's how I met your mother. And I've never looked back."

Sam Grobart nodded, as if in agreement with himself.

David jerked up. "Dad, I have no idea what you're talking about," he said, and fled the room. His father remained in his chair, laughing quietly to himself.

Patch says good-bye to all that

Leaving took forever. Everyone was crying, and the whole deck was littered with suitcases and backpacks and purses and gifts. An unusually large number of people whose names Patch couldn't remember wanted to hug him good-bye, and he went along with it for as long as he could. Finally he had made it to the exit ramp, and was swallowed up in Barker's arms.

"Good luck to you, my boy," he said. "You have been a very special kind of student."

"Uh, thanks," Patch said. "Thanks for everything."

"You must keep in touch."

"Okay."

"Take this," Barker said, beaming. He handed Patch a very large nonfunctional-looking compass. "So you never lose your way."

"Thanks," Patch said. For a minute, he wasn't sure what to do with the unwieldy thing, but then he managed to jam it into his bag. He tried to smile, but Patch always had a hard time smiling when he didn't really mean it. Stephanie came from behind Barker, where she had been hugging some girls good-bye. She was wearing dark glasses.

She leaned in and kissed Patch on the cheek. "I'll never forget you," she whispered.

"Okay," he said. Barker kissed Greta on the check, but Stephanie hung behind. And then Patch and Greta walked off the ship and into London.

"That was a bit much," Greta said as they stepped onto solid land.

Greta snuggled up against him in the cab. The rain had stopped, and even though it was cold, the sky was pretty clear. It was dusk, and they were leaving.

When the cab dropped them at Heathrow, they stood in silence for a moment.

"So . . . what flight are you on?"

"Um," Patch fumbled with his ticket. "Flight 1541."

Greta looked down at her ticket and smiled. "Me, too. I guess I have a layover in New York."

"Are you serious? That's so weird and cool. I get you for a few more hours."

"Yeah, but we're not sitting together."

"I'll just ask them to move you."

"From coach to first class? I don't think they'll do that."

"Come on."

They found a ticket agent, and Patch explained their situation. He grinned like he owned the place, sending the girls behind the counter into fits of giggles.

"I'm sure we can accommodate you," the agent said, winking bawdily at Greta. "Let's see . . . Patch Flood, seat Three-A. It looks like the seat next to yours hasn't been claimed yet. I'm sure we can make the switch, you'll just have to wait until boarding time. Just to be sure that passenger doesn't show up. Why don't you have a seat in our first-class lounge, right over there."

"Thanks," Patch said.

"Thank you," Greta added, still a little bit stunned.

They found the lounge and sat down. "Um, you want a drink or something?"

From the other side of the room, someone called, "Is that Patch?" and someone else, "Patch *Flood?*"

Patch turned, and there were Mickey and Arno.

"What the fuck are you *doing* here?" Arno asked.

"Shouldn't I be asking you guys that?" Patch said softly. "You guys are okay?"

They both nodded, and then watched in awkward surprise as Greta came up behind Patch, wrapping her arms around him. "Hey . . . ," she said shyly, "I hope you guys aren't mad at me for, you know, coming between you."

Arno kind of laughed, because a time when that

could happen seemed very far away now. "Naw . . . ," he said as quickly as he could. Everyone stood around awkwardly, until a voice came over the loudspeaker announcing that first-class passengers could board Flight 1541.

I may actually board an airplane

The ticket agent at Heathrow looked at me like she was looking through me.

"You mean you haven't got your tickets?" she said. "You're going to have to talk to my supervisor."

"But you're the third person I've talked to," I pleaded.

The girl shrugged and walked away. I bugged my eyes at Suki, like, *"Can you believe this shit?"* She looked back at me blankly. All around us was the futuristic echo of arrival and departure, hellos and good-byes.

I had made her leave my dad's house before the butler could serve us dinner, so that we could get on the flights home we had booked before the trip began. Of course, we'd left our tickets on the boat, so I knew it was going to be a headache getting us on a plane. I had insisted we get there two hours early. Suki had protested that that really wasn't her style, but I was adamant. By chance, though, Suki was on the same flight as I was, which was good. We wasted the two hours waiting on various lines and getting nowhere with three different ticket agents. Suki had mentioned several times that she was cranky.

Eventually, another ticketing person came out. She looked older, and more official, so my hopes rose for a moment.

"Tickets, please . . ." she said curtly.

"Um, we haven't got them. But look, we're booked on flight 1541 to New York. I can tell you our seat numbers and—"

"What do you mean you haven't got your tickets?"

"Look, I've explained this to three people already . . ."

"Don't get smart with me, young man."

Suki elbowed me. I could tell she thought this was funny, and I couldn't tell whether that or the ticket agent irritated me more.

"Names . . ."

We gave her our names, and she typed for what seemed like an inordinately long time.

"You don't have your tickets, and you show up ten minutes before the flight takes off . . . ?"

The color drained from my face. "We've been here for two hours," I said in a very small voice.

The agent grunted. "Well, there's nothing I can do."

"Please . . ."

"Well, I suppose Miss Davison can board, because she has an e-ticket. But you, lovey, have a paper ticket without which you cannot board." She sniffed. "Also, due to your lateness, we have given your seat away."

"But . . ." I cursed my mother for being so old-fashioned. She had insisted I buy a paper ticket, the way she insisted I get those useless traveler's checks.

The agent started typing again. She raised her eyes slowly to mine. "I can arrange for you to purchase another seat, in coach, next to Miss Davison."

"But I never fly coach," I said, realizing immediately that this sounded pretentious. But honestly, I've been flying on upgrades from my dad's frequent flyer miles since before I can remember, and once you get used to all the leg room in the first-class cabin, it's really hard to go back.

"Well, princess, you're about to find out how

the people fly. Passports?" We handed them to her, and she looked them over. "You'll have to run."

"Okay."

"That'll be three hundred sixty dollars, then." Suki handed over her card, and we waited breathlessly. A few moments later, the machine made an *Ehhhh* noise.

"Insufficient funds," the agent said impatiently.

"Uh-oh." I looked at Suki.

"I guess I finally ran out," she said. "Those train tickets were kind of expensive."

"Ahem," the agent said, "Miss Davison, if you like, though I don't advise it, because you have an e-ticket, you *could* exchange the second leg of your trip, from JFK to SFO, so the young man can fly with you to New York. You'll have to figure something else out from there, though."

"Okay," I said quickly, and then I whispered to Suki: "When we get to New York, I promise I'll find a way for you to get home. I promise."

"Right," she whispered, rolling her eyes. Then she told the agent that that was fine. The agent printed our tickets and handed them to us with a good-riddance gesture.

302

The airport blurred by us as we hurried to our gate. When we got there, the stewardesses were just about to close the door. They ushered us on, saying, "You're late! All the way down to your left. You'll enter at row eleven, go all the way back and take a left and just keep walking." We hurried through the corridor and into the plane itself. I looked around wildly, thinking maybe, just maybe, I'll recognize a stewardess or something and they'll move me up. But the entrance to the plane was in coach, so as we hurried to our seats I didn't even get a glimpse of the good life.

The guys are reunited in style

"Don't you just love first class?" Sara-Beth Benny was saying as the stewardess handed out mimosas to everyone in the cabin. She had been seated shortly after Mickey, Arno, Patch, and Greta, and she had been talking ever since. Subsequently, none of the guys had really caught up much. "I mean, free drinks for six hours! It's just like when I go to a bar in New York."

Greta was staring at her with her mouth open. She took her mimosa and thanked the stewardess for it excessively.

"I mean, this is *so* nice after that awful trip, right? Wasn't it like *the worst*," Sara-Beth went on.

"Uh-huh."

"I mean, I don't think I left my room after that wild party of yours, Patch. I can barely remember a thing about it, which means it *must* have been good. I woke up with such a headache! And then I just, you know, read magazines in my room as much as possible the rest of the trip. I didn't I miss anything, did I . . . ?"

"Not really," Mickey and Arno said at once.

"Yeah, the last week or so was mostly tests. But Barker exempted me from all of them, so I had nothing to do," Patch said. Then he shrugged and continued on to say, as though it were no big deal, "But I had Greta all to myself, so that was cool."

"Uh-huh," Sara-Beth said, oblivious to the fact that Greta was blushing like crazy, and that Arno and Mickey had straightened awkwardly in their seats. "Oh, hey," she called to the stewardess, swinging around in her seat and waving her empty champagne flute, "could I get another?"

I fly with the people

Outside my window, there was nothing but clouds and the occasional peek of ocean. Suki and I had been playing cards for like two hours. *The Incredibles* was on, but I'd already seen it, and besides, in coach you have to pay for earphones, and once again we had no money. I reflected, not for the first time on this trip, how quickly money seems to go when you don't really have it. Also, Suki had declared the movie "Trash that rots your brain," even though it still looked funny to me, and that had basically closed the issue.

One thing that is free, no matter what, on international flights, is drinks. So I ordered us each a Bloody Mary and then we felt much better. We were sort of starting to have fun again, but something had definitely changed. It was like we were sidestepping each other, inasmuch as you can when you are sitting very close to each other in very cramped economy airplane seats and playing gin. Suki wasn't even really gloating when she scored points. To be honest, I had been thinking about Flan ever since I got this new look into Rob's life, and I couldn't really take Suki seriously after that. Maybe she sensed this, somehow. When she won, she smiled at me faintly and said, "Good game." Then she turned away from me, wrapped herself up in the airplane blanket, and went to sleep.

I realize I should probably have tried to talk to Suki right then, but I just couldn't. Instead I waited until I knew she was asleep, and then I went through her bag. I borrowed her bank card and used it to log onto the Internet on the little TV screen in front of my seat.

Watching the page open, I wasn't as anxious as usual, but I was filled with a more real kind of worry. Not surprisingly, there was nothing from Flan and one message from David and one from Rob. I decided to face the worst first.

From: santananumerouno@yahoo.com
To: jonathanm@gissing.edu

Dear Jon: I am so apologizing I forgot to send you by e-mail your mother's number at the ranch. And now I cannot find it, oopsie! But I am sure that with the money I wired, you made it safe to my home in London, and soon will be coming home to New York. I am sure my butler mother you like crazy no? I love that man! New York is crazy. Why did you ever leave?! Your mother hasn't been back from the ranch yet, but I have been mostly at the Floods house. So much fun there. That girl is so sexy and crazy! She has really taken me to her bosom. –ROB

Her *bosom?* Who they hell was this guy? My anxiety level increased, of course, and I considered asking the stewardess if she could speed the plane up. I opened up the e-mail from David.

From: grobman@hotmail.com
To: jonathanm@gissing.edu

Hey man. I found Rob, but your mom's still out of town and no one can figure out the number to reach her. Sorry. I haven't heard from you in a while. You OK? When are you coming home? We should talk about some things. I've been talking to my dad a lot since I came home early from the trip. I know he's kind of a kook about feelings and stuff but I had a lot of issues after that. And I sort of talked to him about the thing you asked me about with Flan and Rob, just to see if it was like normal. And my dad made me see a lot of things. Anyway don't worry—I'm pretty sure that Rob isn't, like, interested in Flan. But maybe you shouldn't be either, you know what I mean? See you, David

I shut down my e-mail account and slipped Suki's bank card back into her bag. I was almost woozy trying to figure out what those e-mails meant. Clearly David was just trying to make me feel better: Rob had seduced my perfect little Flan. I rang the stewardess for another Bloody Mary. Suki was still sleeping peacefully beside me, and as I looked at her I realized the one thing I wasn't going to do until I was back in New York: sleep peacefully.

A few last moments suspended in air

The stewardesses in first class had finally gotten wise and cut Sara-Beth off. Luckily for them, it was right around the time that she fell into a champagne coma and began softly humming the *Mike's Princesses* theme song in her sleep.

In the two seats next to and opposite her, her former Ocean Term classmates were being served liqueurs. As they sipped them, Mickey talked about Angelina and the house in Barcelona, and the Lober-Luccis and how creepy it was that they had known Barker in college. And Greta told them how boring and uneventful the rest of the trip was, and how she had gotten sick and she and Patch had been excused from all the papers and tests they were supposed to have in the final week. She skipped over the part about them hooking up, though, and avoided entirely the nasty scene with Stephanie. The stewardess brought a second round, and then Arno said, "So, I guess Jonathan and Suki never made it back to the boat?"

"Yeah, it was weird," Patch said. "I mean, weird because they didn't figure out to show up back at the boat. And weird because . . . well, I guess because it's Jonathan."

"Yeah. He'll be fine, though," Mickey said. "I mean, he probably just got his mom or his dad or PISS to wire him money, right? I mean, he's probably in New York already, buying back-to-school clothes or some shit."

They all laughed a little bit and then fell silent. After a few beats, Arno said, "Oh, Mickey forgot to tell you this weird thing about Angelina's. We met this guy, who was, like, a performance artist supposedly, and he was wearing a watch just like Jonathan's." Arno reached into his pocket and took it out so that they could all see. "I mean, isn't it just like J's?" he asked Patch.

"I guess . . ."

"Anyway, we took it as a souvenir. You never know, maybe it really is J's."

Patch took the watch out of Arno's hand and turned it over. "Well, it does have his initials engraved on the back."

"Oh . . . ," they all said at once, and then fell silent again.

Outside their windows, the sky and the Atlantic Ocean had gone dark. They all sunk back into the big, comfy, shark-gray leather first-class seats, and drifted into their own thoughts. All the way up there in the air, at the mercy of stewardesses and weather, it was pretty hard to stave off thoughts of homecoming and what that meant. Patch wondered about that e-mail from David about Selina Trieff, and if he was even interested in her anymore now that he'd been with Greta. Arno wondered if he and Mickey were going to be able to maintain the closeness they'd developed over the last two days. Also, he wondered if his appeal to girls was totally gone, and what life would be like without that. Mickey wondered if Arno was going to be able to keep being decent to him, or if the rest of their friendship was going to be spent sparring over chicks. They all thought about Jonathan, and where he could be, and if they would all still be friends if something terrible had happened.

Greta wondered if Patch really liked her, and Sara-Beth twisted in her sleep and hoped in her dreams that, someday, she would have a career again.

They were heading back to New York, and for the moment none of them really knew what that meant.

Everything moves roughly in the direction of normal

As the plane began to come down through the atmosphere for landing, I checked the weather and my seat belt and whatever else I could to be busy. I was landing on home turf, but I had no idea what to expect. Plus, at this point I was pretty sure Suki and I were both feeling a little sheepish about our night in Mallorca. When the taxiing was done, and the lights were back on, I picked up Suki's bag and mine. It took us a long time to get out because we were all the way at the back of the plane.

Once we'd made our way out of the airport, I saw that the little screen in the plane had told the truth. It was a cold and crisp evening in New York. The sky was already dark, and the cars made orange streaks in the purple night.

"How is it possible that during the warmest winter on record in Europe, it is so freaking cold in New York?" I asked.

"Global warming," Suki said brightly. "It's a really huge problem, and nobody pays any attention. I mean, if you only knew how—"

"C'mon, let's get a cab," I said, interrupting her and dragging her by the arm to the taxi line.

"But aren't we out of money again?" She seemed thankfully to have forgotten about her global warming speech.

"Yeah, but the doorman will front me. I've known him since I was five."

We got in line and were sort of silent and introverted for a while, wrapping ourselves up in the coats that PISS's butler had lent us. They were too big, and they made us look like hobos, but I guess it was good that we had them because, according to the little screen, it was in the mid-thirties. That was when I heard some familiar voices up ahead.

A girl was saying, ". . . I'm really glad you asked me to extend the layover and stay. I mean, thank you, I . . ."

And then this guy's voice, which was kind of hoarse and slow, said, "Hey, stop worrying. It's going to be fun."

Very near them, someone was talking into a

cell phone and saying, "Okay, Mom, love you, too. I'll see you tomorrow." Then he hung up and said, "You'll never believe it, but I don't think they know. I don't think Caselli ever told them. And if they don't know now, they ain't never findin' out. Woooohhhhhooooo!!!" That was definitely Mickey, and although I wasn't sure exactly what he was talking about, the context of Mickey sort of explained it all. And beside him, Patch and Greta and Arno.

"Hey!" I yelled. "Hey, it's Jonathan. And Suki."

Everyone in line between me and my friends turned to look at us. "Don't think there's any cutting, because there isn't," the woman in front of me said, wagging her finger.

"What are you, in kindergarten?" I snarled. I grabbed Suki's hand, and we hurried past the ten or so people in line between us and them. Everybody grumbled, but nobody did anything, which is totally typical New Yorker behavior.

When we got to Mickey and Arno and Greta and Patch, we all just stared at each other for a minute because it was way too weird. Then Arno raised his eyes slowly and strangely to mine, because Suki and I were holding hands again. I let go. To break the silence I said, "So . . . you guys want to, like, share a cab?" And whatever the awkwardness was, that ended it. We started hugging and yelling questions at each other and everyone was talking at once. If there were people still pissed at us back in the line, we couldn't hear them now.

Suki and Greta sort of withdrew to the side and were whispering to each other. I looked at the guys and said, "Someone explain to me how we brought these two back with us . . . ?"

"Oh, Greta had a layover," Patch said, as if that explained it. Then he added, "And I, you know, asked her to stay."

"Bitch, *you're* the one with explainin' to do," Mickey said, although I had a feeling this wasn't entirely true.

We got one of those minivan cabs and put our stuff in and crowded into the seats. Just as I was about to close the door, I heard somebody calling out to us. I looked up and saw Sara-Beth Benny standing next to a limo, looking very fashionably wintry. She was blowing us kisses. We all waved, and she waved and got into her car and was gone. It was surreal, but pretty much everything seemed surreal right then.

Then I slammed the door, and somebody told

the driver how to get to Patch's. It just seemed like the natural thing to do. As we rode through Queens I started telling them all the things that had happened to us since that day in Mallorca. For the first time, it started to seem kind of funny.

By the time we drove across the Williamsburg Bridge, and on to Delancey, we all knew how we had spent our days apart. "Thank God we're back in Manhattan," I said. "I feel like never leaving again. And none of you are allowed to, either." Everyone murmured in agreement. And even though Greta and Suki were in the car, and even though that was pretty much cool with us, my guys knew who I was talking about.

Arno goes after what he likes

"Sounds like we're approaching the Flood residence," Arno said dryly.

As the cab turned the corner onto Perry Street, they heard music coming out of the Floods' town house. It sounded like The Detroit Cobras, or something else that February would play. It was definitely a February party.

Arno, who had been sitting in the front seat, said "I'll get it," and began looking around for his wallet. He was feeling sort of low. Whatever was up with his relative non-attractiveness to girls, he didn't like it. The Greta thing, he had to admit, was mostly a continuation of his competition with Mickey. But Suki he was actually into, and seeing her holding hands with Jonathan stung. Maybe she was just the hand-holding type—it wasn't a type he was really familiar with. Paying for the car gave him an edge, though, and as he followed the rest of them up to the door, he started to feel back in his game.

They all stood there for a minute, and then Arno said, "Hey, Patch, wanna let us in?"

"I forgot my key." Patch shrugged. He rang the doorbell, but nobody could hear it because the music was too loud. Patch threw his head back and yelled, "Flan! Feb! Let us in!"

For a while, it didn't look like anyone was coming. But then the door swung back and February Flood stood in the doorway. Her hair was wild and her mascara was smudged all around her eyes. She was wearing a black slip that was much too big for her and lace-up high-heeled ankle boots without the laces, and she was smoking a cigarette. It was hard to tell if she had just gotten laid, or if she was just dressed that way. "Oh goody," she said flatly, looking at Patch, "you're home."

Everyone trooped into the front room, where it was very dark and very loud. It sounded like there were a lot of people in the living room and in the rooms beyond.

"I got in a fight with Mom and Dad," February was saying as the guys hung up their coats and shoved their luggage into one of the hallway closets. "I don't even remember what it was about, but they were being total assholes and they went to vacation, to this place called Mallorca. Heard of it?"

Jonathan looked like he was about to be hysterical,

and Suki actually did laugh. "You mean, in Spain?"

"Yeah, Spain. Who the hell are you?"

"That's just really funny because—" Suki started to say, but February interrupted with a terse, "Whatever. So I decided to have a party. Hope you don't, you know, mind."

Patch introduced Greta and Suki to February, who looked like she was probably going to forget their names as soon as they were gone.

Just then David and Rob came down the stairs. February turned to them and said, "Where's Flan?"

Jonathan's face went pale and his jaw dropped as his friend and stepbrother descended from the direction of Flan's room. David's face was all twisted up, like he didn't know whether to be happy or sad that all his friends were back. But Rob looked euphoric. He was wearing a suit vest, a tie, Diesel jeans, and nothing else. As he came down the stairs he held up a bottle and cried, "Welcome," as though it were his house.

To everyone's surprise, Jonathan ran at him with his fist clenched. Rob didn't seem to register what was going on, as though he couldn't comprehend why anyone would be mad at him. Luckily for Rob, the swing went slightly to the right of his head, although Jonathan had gotten enough momentum going that when they collided, they went crashing to the floor.

"You asshole!" Jonathan was shouting as he Rob rolled on the floor pummeling each other. By this time, Rob seemed to have caught on and was hitting back. "How could you move in on my life like that? How could you corrupt my little Flan?"

Everyone gasped, although they basically all knew how Jonathan felt about her. It was more just hearing him call her "my Flan" loudly and front of everyone while he was tussling with his new stepbrother.

David, who had been inching along the wall, finally reached Arno. They said "what's up" and hugged awkwardly without taking their eyes off of Jonathan. "What the fuck's happening here?" Arno asked.

David shook his head, sort of unconvincingly. "I dunno."

Finally February, who had been clapping her hands and enjoying the whole melee, had had enough. She reached in and grabbed Jonathan by the collar and pulled him up on his feet.

"Okay, cowboy," she said, "get off my date." Everyone gasped again. February hissed at them, hauling Jonathan over toward David and Arno. She grabbed David's collar with her other hand, which looked especially ridiculous, since David was so tall. "And you, loverboy," she said to David, "time for you two good old buddies to have a nice little chat."

David turned to Arno, with a plaintive help-me expression. Arno smirked. Whatever was going on here was too good to stop. As David was being pulled away, though, Arno reached into his pocket and pulled out Jonathan's watch. He put it in the hand that David was reaching out toward him, and said, "This might help you." Then February pushed them down the stairs and into the kitchen and kicked all the random people there out. When she came back into the hallway, she helped Rob up, and they disappeared up the stairs.

"That is seriously weird," Arno said to Mickey. They looked over to where Greta and Suki were whispering, and they knew that by then Suki knew everything about the survival test. Patch walked over to them and took Greta by the hand and led her up the stairs. "Why don't you guys come to the roof?" he called down to them.

Arno looked at Suki, then back at Mickey. "Hey dude, I don't want to fight with you. But I think I like her."

"Yeah, I know," Mickey said. "Go on. She picked you anyway."

Once Mickey had gone up to the roof, Arno went over to where Suki was standing by herself. "Hey," he said, "sorry all this craziness got in the way. But I think something was going to finally happen between us that day on Mallorca . . ."

"Yeah, I thought so, too," Suki said, smiling. "You keep on having a face like that, and it just might."

Now that I'm in Flan's house, I'm further away from her than ever

February had cleared everybody out of the kitchen, and now it was just me and David sitting across from each other at the big, industrial-looking table. I rubbed my shoulder, which was hurting because I'd fallen on it, and stared at David. He was hanging his head.

"What's up with you, man? Your e-mails got really weird, and like, sort of mean. Are you mad at me?" I said, because even though I urgently wanted to know where Flan was, and what was going on, part of me just wanted all the bad feelings to go away and for Flan to be pure and safe. At least I knew she wasn't with Rob, who February was obviously, if very bizarrely, into. And that meant he definitely was not and had never seriously been interested in her little sister.

David raised his eyes to me. "Not really anymore. I mean, I was. Not at you, but at all of you guys. It's probably not really fair, but I feel like you guys were really shitty after I got kicked off the boat."

"But I was the only one who e-mailed you!"

"I know. My dad says I have shoot-the-messenger syndrome, or some shit." We both laughed at that, even though it really wasn't funny. "Anyway, Rob's not interested in Flan—"

"I can see that—"

"—I am."

"Oh," I said. The room sort of went blurry, and if someone had asked me my name I'm not sure I could have told them. I said, "Oh," again, although I'm not sure I got the whole word out.

"I just . . . After you asked me to 'keep an eye on her for you,' I started hanging around her a lot. And since Rob was my only friend in New York, and he was hanging out with Feb, it made sense. Flan was, like, really comforting. She's sharp, and she said all these really smart things about our dynamic as a group and it . . . made me feel okay."

"Oh." I felt like my insides had been pulled out. These were all things I knew about Flan already. My Flan. If I'd wanted to beat Rob to a pulp, now all I wanted to do was not be. This was so infinitely worse.

"My dad told me this story about how he met my mom in college. He said the same thing happened. This buddy of his was going out with Mom, and he went abroad for his junior year, and when he came back my dad and mom were engaged. It made me feel like it might be kind of romantic if . . ."

"Oh," I said, because whatever he was going to say, I didn't want to hear it.

"But then I realized that that's my parents, and that's fucking gross. Anyway, I didn't do anything with Flan. I just thought about it. And that's not so hard to believe, right? Flan's a really cool kid. In fact, she's not really a kid at all. She's fucking hot, and if you want to be with her you should tell her and stop saying one thing and doing another."

I took a deep breath, and for a minute I thought I might cry. Whatever mangle of emotions I had experienced with Suki on the beach, this was much, much more intense.

"What are you, my therapist?" I said, smiling suddenly out of sheer relief.

"I'm sorry, man," David said, giving me a very earnest look. "I'm glad you're back, but we can talk all this shit out later. Right now, you better go find Flan."

I stood up, still not entirely sure how to feel about anything. David reached out his hand and we shook in this really stilted way. I felt something cold and metallic in his hand, and when I pulled my hand away I saw that he had palmed me a watch. My watch, the Tiffany's one with my initials engraved in the back.

"How did you get this?" I asked.

"Don't ask," he said. And even though the whole thing was improbable, I was so overcome by the miraculousness of it all, that I threw my arms around him and we hugged in a really sincere way.

"I missed you, dude," I said, " and I'll see you really, really soon."

"Go," he said, and I went off to find Flan.

But I don't go to Flan's room, not straightaway

I took the stairs two at a time up to the roof. It was still kind of early, for New York, and all of February's friends, and all their friends and friends' friends, were still crowding the stairwells and most of the rooms on the first floor. It was strangely quiet up on the roof, and you could tell that everybody down below thought it was still winter, when in fact the air was kind of temperate and refreshing and clear. All of the plants were sill brown and leafless, of course, but they looked nice against that pale lavender color that you only get in a city as crazy and twisted and lit up as New York.

There were a few people up there I didn't know, and then some people I knew really well. Patch and Greta were standing over by the railing looking into the garden. Greta was wearing this white velvet blazer that I think I recognized from Flan's closet, and it complemented her hair really nicely. She looked kind of sophisticated, which I realized was something that I never really thought of Flan as being. But now, looking at her coat on another girl, I realized that I actually, subconsciously, knew this all along. Arno and Suki were leaning up against another part of the railing. He had his coat spread over both their shoulders, and he was nibbling at her ear. As I looked at them I realized I didn't feel weird about Suki at all, and also that they looked great together. Farther down the railing, February and Rob were doing something disgusting with their tongues. They didn't exactly make as beautiful a couple, but it was something I guess I was going to have to get used to.

"What are you doing up here?" Greta had turned and was calling out to me. I walked over to her and Patch, and Suki and Arno came over, too.

"I don't know, I just wanted to say good night, I guess. In case you guys all disappeared. I mean, where's Mickey gone off to already?"

"He got lonely, I guess," Patch said, and he pointed across the gardens to the Fradys' roof, where Mickey and Philippa were . . . talking.

"Yeah, you just can't keep those crazy kids apart."

"Speaking of which, what are you doing up here?" Arno said, giving me that look he always gives me when he thinks he can teach me something about girls. I didn't mind, though; it was just in his nature to act like that. And he probably *had* taught me a lot about girls, so who could blame him?

Suki disentangled herself from Arno and walked over to me. She laced her arm in mine, and for a minute I thought she was going to do something really embarrassing, like confess her love to me or tell all my friends that we'd made out on a beach in the moonlight. (Which was seeming cheesier every time I thought about it.) But she didn't. She said, "Jonathan, say good night to your friends," in this very mothering tone.

"Good night, friends," I said sort of jokily, and waved.

"Good night," everyone said.

Suki walked me back over to the stairs. "Patch just introduced Greta and me to his little sister," she said. This felt weird, but I was trying to go with it. "She's really a catch; we both thought so . . . Hey, Jonathan? I had some fun with you on our little trip. I even had fun kissing you, but we

331

don't have to tell anybody that part, right? Because the thing is . . . I knew, when you told me about Flan, in the hostel in Mallorca, that you really, really liked her. And I think you guys make a good couple. Now go tell her you missed her, you jerk!" Then she ran back over to Arno, and I waved at my friends one last time and walked down the stairs to Flan's room.

There was no one in the hall now, and I knocked lightly. After a few minutes I hadn't heard anything, so I knocked again. I waited, trying to breathe steadily, to the point where I was going to have to barge in or give up. But then I heard the soft, sweet voice of Flan Flood, close to the other side of the door. She was saying, "If that's Jonathan, you can't come in."

I put my forehead against the door. "Hey, Flan. I know I said some stupid shit . . . but I traveled on boats, and slow trains, and shitty cramped airplanes, all the way across the ocean, to see you. And I missed you really, really bad, and . . ."

The door opened, and there was Flan, with her golden hair undone and wearing nothing but an XL Guns N' Roses shirt that looked like it used to be black. She shook her head and said, "God you're hokey."

But she was smiling, too, in this sweet, mysterious way that was hard to decipher. I took her hand and slipped my watch onto her wrist. It made her wrist look tiny, but it also made her look tough, and older. "You have no idea how hard it was to bring that back here to you," I said, even though I didn't really have any idea, either.

"Thank you," she mouthed, twisting it around her wrist. Then she put her hands around my neck, and kept giving me that smile. I wasn't sure what it meant, but I was sure I wanted to find out.

Don't miss the next Insiders book—*Break Every Rule*!

It's spring in New York and things are heating up:

Jonathan's torn between his demanding girlfriend and his guys.

Mickey gets into photography—the naked kind!

Arno is named Hottest Private School Boy . . . but can he handle the title?

Patch is suddenly desperate to reconnect with a girl from his past—if he can find her!

And David falls for the ultimate anti-It Girl. Could it be love?

While you wait, check out what's new with the guys at www.insidersbook.com.